The Elephants' Child

M. L. Eaton

A lonely English girl discovers love and
friendship in 1950's India

Published by Touchworks Ltd.
a company registered in England, no. 03668464.
Registered Office: 67 London Road, St. Leonards-on-Sea,
East Sussex TN37 6AR.

Also by M L Eaton

Mysterious Marsh series
#1 When the Clocks Stopped
#2 When the Tide Turned

Faraway Lands series
#1 The Elephants' Child
#2 The Lion Mountains

Short Read
Norfolk Twilight

All books available in print and as e-books from Amazon including amazon.co.uk, amazon.com, amazon.com.au and amazon.in

A catalogue record for this title is available from the British Library.

- For -

Dhivya Balaji and *Shree Janani Sundararajan*

with admiration and gratitude

'Om Gum Ganapatayei Namaha'

'Salutations to Ganesh, the remover of obstacles'

One of the mantras of Ganesha, the elephant-headed god, the embodiment of wisdom and bliss.

Lord Ganesha is the sage, the master of knowledge, protector of all beings and guardian of beauty, prosperity, grace and compassion.
As the guardian of the doors of houses and temple, he removes both internal and external obstacles to success and grants the opening of spiritual gifts.

- 1 -

Prologue

A gush of air bore the animal's spirit from her body. The earth quaked with the shock: after-tremors rocked the trees, rustling their leaves. Silence: bending trees slowly straightening. In the aftermath of death there was a great stillness. Even the calf was still now, frozen in shock as well as bound in ropes, silent in its cage. The silence stretched: and stretched further. Until slowly, slowly, men crept out from behind trees and undergrowth. Others descended from the treetops. The white man, who had fallen full length upon the ground, slowly rose and gathered up his gun.

Silent in her prison, the elephant calf grieved for her mother, her freedom, her kind. Never again, she intuited, would she be free to roam the green and sacred land. Never again would she watch a lazy bird-of-prey circle between the green jungle hills; never again would she play with her kind in the crystal waters of the creeks — squirting water, bathing, drinking, playing. Ever after, she would be at the mercy of man, this puny creature who would beat and poke the spirit from her, until she did his bidding always.

When Melanie woke in the morning the dream was still upon her. A great weight crushed against her heart and she felt the agony of mother and child in every pore of her being, but she did not weep for the grief was too deep, too real for tears. And today was the day her mother was going away. It was her grief too.

- 2 -

Kent, England. 1951

When she was a tiny girl of about three and three quarters, her father told Melanie about elephants. She was happily seated on his knee and they had been playing 'This is the way the ladies ride' and laughing until they were breathless.

Then he had changed the game and made it more exciting. *Really* exciting! They played 'riding a nelephant'. Instead of pretending that his lap was a horse, she was on his shoulders and he was rocking from side to side, lifting up one foot and then the other, one arm holding her safe and the other dangling in front like an elephant's nose.

Elephants, Daddy said, were huge creatures: grey and wrinkly with incredibly long noses that they used like fingers. Fancy if you could pick flowers with your nose! Or pick an apple off a tree and eat it, using only your nose? An elephant's nose was so long that it could pick things up off the ground without bending down and could reach up to get the juiciest leaves from the top of a tree. Of course, it wasn't called a nose. It was called a 'trunk' and he said that was because, being grey and wrinkly like the rest of the elephant, it looked like a tree trunk. Melanie found it hard to think that anything could have such a huge long nose, but if her father said so — and if he *promised* it was true and *promised* that he wasn't teasing her — then it must be true. She quietly decided that she would ask Jesus to make her into a 'nelephant', just to surprise her father — and a day or so later he discovered his little daughter crawling around on the carpet trying to pick up a biscuit with her nose. She had taken one look at him and burst into fretful tears, saying that she had prayed and prayed and *prayed* to grow big like a nelephant with a nose like an nelephant but it was no good! She'd pulled and pulled at her nose but she *still* couldn't pick anything up with it.

Her father tried not to laugh; but Melanie could see the grin trying to get out of his mouth and she was furious! How could he laugh at her? Not being a nelephant was so very, *very* annoying. She stamped her foot and turned her back on him, until he wheedled her into turning round by promising to tell her more about elephants.

Daddy said that elephants could do other things with their nose-trunks. What did she think those things might be? Melanie thought for a moment and said that perhaps elephants would breathe through their noses, because that was what she did with her nose most of the time, though they might only use it for sneezing which was really breathing going the wrong way and making a lot of noise. Daddy said yes they did use their noses for breathing but he had never heard an elephant sneeze — and he was glad because it was an awful lot of nose to sneeze through. But his eyes were twinkling and she thought he was probably still laughing at her.

She demanded to know what else elephants did with

their trunks and he said they stroked their babies with their trunks, they sniffed up water through their trunks and then blew it out over their backs like a shower, and sometimes they threw their trunks right up high — he demonstrated this using an arm — and made a hullabaloo of a noise out of it, a high-pitched squeal that was called 'trumpeting'. Melanie had no idea what 'high-pitched' meant but she knew what a squeal was.

So they both pretended they were elephants and trumpeted all round the sitting room until her mother came in and told them to stop because they were giving her a headache; and anyway supper was ready for her father and Melanie's bath was drawn and waiting for her.

But then it got really exciting! Daddy asked Mummy to put his supper back in the oven because he wanted to bath Melanie. He did, and they played showering elephants. Melanie spluttered and nearly drowned when she breathed the water up, so they used her toy watering can instead and his shirt got soaked through and the floor got very, very wet. And her mother came in and said she was 'exceedingly' cross — which meant 'very' but sounded much worse. Melanie could see that she wasn't really cross because she kissed Daddy and told him *she* would put Melanie to bed 'pronto' because his supper was all dried up from being in the oven for so long.

Her father said goodnight and went downstairs in his wet shirt which was all sticking to him and Melanie was so disappointed that she started to cry. Wrapping her daughter in the big towel she had warmed on the kitchen range, her mother carted her off to bed, but Melanie was still sobbing — which was because she was over-tired, Mummy said, before tickling her until they were both gasping and happy again. Then they had a lovely tight hug and she snuggled Melanie down under the blankets and read her a story from a new book called 'Bar-bar the Elephant'. But Melanie was fast asleep before her mother had read half a page, although she felt her mother's lips kiss her softly, like a whisper, on her brow, and heard her creep out of the room and down the stairs.

That night Melanie's dreams were full of elephants.

- 3 -

Karachi, Pakistan. 1954

Squeezing her little hand in reassurance, her mother bent down to Melanie and whispered: "What do you say?"

The little girl, feeling incredibly shy, kept her eyes cast down. In her hands she held a small handbag made of purple plastic with a shiny heart-shaped piece of silk glued to its side. She touched the silk with her finger, turned the bag so that the silk caught a sunbeam and flashed a million bright colours, and a tear dropped, making a dark splurge on the material. The bag was beautiful — the more beautiful because the Bearer was smiling and saying that he hoped she would remember him. She knew it was a very special gift, one that must have cost the Bearer a lot of money and Mummy had told her that he did not have much money to spend.

She raised her eyes to the dark, bearded man wearing an immaculate white turban and glanced at her mother, who nodded encouragement.

"Thank you, Sundar Singh," she whispered. "It's lovely. But wouldn't your little daughter like it?"

She held it out to him and suddenly his stateliness was gone. His face beamed in a smile of startling whiteness which was all the more shocking to Melanie because she had seldom seen him smile.

He had ruled the household with quiet, serious

efficiency. Always appearing on silent feet when he was required, always stately, tall and retiring. He seldom spoke and, when he did, it was in a calm, soft voice and nearly always in answer to a request or query from her mother.

"No, Missy Baba," he smiled. "It is for *you*. I bought it in the bazaar especially for you. You can take it back to England, Missy Baba."

Inexplicably, because he had always treated her with such a quiet elegance that she had believed that she, too was a memsahib, his hand ruffled her blondish curls.

"But..." she began, and stopped suddenly at her mother's swift half-frown.

She had been going to say that they weren't going back to England, they were going to Bombay in India. And it was true! She felt her lip pouting and trembling. She hated to be reprimanded, even a little, and anyway she didn't want to be called Missy Baba! Couldn't he see that she was a memsahib? He should call her Missy *Memsahib* — not Missy Baba! Baba was what Amy's ayah called Michael and he was only two! She wasn't a baby any more — she was six-and-a-half years old. And she'd always been too old for an ayah, anyway.

Then the tears ran over because she couldn't bear to leave this tall quiet man with his kind brown eyes and his soft voice and gentle ways. Quite forgetting her dignity, she threw her arms round his waist and let the tears flow.

"I don't want to go!" she sobbed. "I want to stay here with you, and the papayas, and the dhobi, and Kelly, and the driver and the r...rabbits. And even with Cook."

The Bearer, more surprised than shocked at this sudden show of emotion, gently disentangled her arms and took a step back. Although she was elegantly be-suited and hatted ready for the journey, Melanie's mother squatted down beside her daughter and gently wiped the tears away with a lace handkerchief.

"I know. We're all sad to leave, darling. But we *have* to go now. You must be brave and stop crying. You have to learn to be a lady — and ladies don't cry. There! That's better." She stood up, stowing the handkerchief back in her handbag while Melanie did her best not to sniff too hard and to try to be a lady.

She lifted her chin and essayed a smile, but her eyelashes were stuck together with tears as she regarded the servants whom the Bearer had lined up on the veranda to bid goodbye to their employers.

It was the custom: just as it was the custom for those employers, who had already paid the servants their wages and given them each a few extra rupees, to say a formal goodbye and leave the Bearer with a sum to share out amongst his staff according to the time-honoured fashion of the Raj. Not that it was the Raj now, Melanie knew. It was 1954 and she was vaguely aware that something had happened about the time she was born, in 1947, so that now this bit of India was called Pakistan.

Melanie didn't like goodbyes. She remembered how sad it was when, eighteen months previously, she and her parents had left England for Karachi. They had said goodbye to her big brother, Trevor, who had been born a long time ago — *before* the war — and was going to a place called university, which seemed to be an interesting place full of animals. He was training to be an animal doctor, although it had a funny name, something like Vet-in-ry Surgeon.

Then she had to say goodbye to her favourite cousins: Anne, who was three months younger than her with black curls instead of fair and she didn't suck her thumb *ever*; and Jane, who was a very small girl of three with a huge grin and an irritating habit of asking 'why?' all the time. At least, Daddy said it was 'an irritating habit', but Melanie thought Jane just wanted to know things. And it had been goodbye, too, to the big rambling farmhouse with all the cats and dogs where they all lived — Mummy, Daddy, Trevor, Melanie, Anne, Jane, Aunt Evelyn, Uncle Paul and Grandpa.

She missed Anne most because Jane was a bit annoying, always tagging along behind — and she would never eat her sweets fast enough, so Melanie and Anne would have to watch her sucking them when theirs were all finished.

But, Trevor, her big brother, was the most special of them all. He used to walk around with Melanie on his shoulders and tell her to catch a bit of the sky and then to put it back so she wouldn't be sucked into Heaven before her time; and he taught her naughty rhymes which were *their special secret* from Mummy and Daddy; and he had even been teaching her to play cricket, although the bat was too big for her to hold properly. She missed him *terribly.* Trevor had bought her a special doll to take with her. *'Her name's Matilda'* he'd said when he gave it to her, *'She needs a Mummy to take care of her.'*

Mummy had smiled when they said goodbye. Melanie had tried to be brave and smile too, but not very successfully. She had cried into the doll's dress all the way to the ship until it was soggy all down the front. Mummy and Daddy were pretending to be happy, but she knew they were sad, too. Adults were such peculiar things: they pretended nearly *all* the time. Melanie thought that must be 'exhausting' as Mummy would say — it meant 'very tired' but sounded much worse.

Those goodbyes had been a long time ago. She had eventually settled into her new life in Pakistan, but the overwhelming feeling of loss had come back to her yesterday when she had said goodbye to Karachi Grammar School and to the friends she had made there.

Today she had already said goodbye to Kelly, the dog with the tail that curled tightly over his back, and to her beloved white rabbits. In fact, she had been round the house and said goodbye to all the rooms; then she had gone outside and said goodbye to all the flowers she had planted; waved at the horseradish that had grown from a small piece her mother had smuggled in from England — and that was now fanning out towards the railway line in the Sindh desert where nothing else ever grew; she'd even gone into the servants' part of the garden and said goodbye to the bantam hens as well as to the chilli bushes and the little bed of herbs that Cook nurtured.

She frowned. She used to like Cook — although his brow was always beaded with sweat and he wore a grey singlet that smelled, especially under the arms — because he had a wide smile and used to make intricate tiny baskets of spun sugar full of sugared almonds, especially for her. The baskets were so pretty that she could hardly bear to eat them, but once she had eaten the almonds, she would break off a tiny bit of the basket (just to taste) and, before long, the whole basket had dissolved on her tongue. She *used* to like Cook — but that was before she had found the dead white rabbit on the countertop in the kitchen.

She had first seen the white rabbits in the bazaar where she would go sometimes with her mother, who enjoyed driving a mutually satisfying bargain for the wonderful materials that the derzi would later sew into dresses that swished and fluttered delightfully. Melanie had an especial favourite among her mother's evening dresses — a strapless creation of straw-coloured silk. The beautiful gown fell to the floor in many folds from a ruched bodice, to which was attached a long stole that was designed to be flung carelessly over the shoulder so as to trail down behind. She loved the evenings when her mother would come in to kiss her goodnight on the way out to a 'do', floating in on a cloud of perfume, her high heels clicking on the floor.

Melanie loved the bazaar too, with its myriad of amazing colours and its heady mixture of scents from aniseed and sandalwood to the pungent odour of donkey's ordure, mixed with the smell of fish, people and motor exhaust fumes. But sometimes she found the whole thing overwhelming: the live chickens hung up by their feet; little white rabbits with pink noses and red eyes penned up in tiny enclosures; songbirds crammed into bird cages. Then she would drag her mother by the hand close to the poor animals, squat in the dust and sing to make them feel better. She knew they didn't like being cooped up in cages in the hot, dusty, noisy bazaar, so she saved up all her pocket money — which was only a few rupees — to buy the freedom of birds and rabbits. She would have liked to buy all the hens too but they were too expensive.

She set the birds free as soon as they were home, although she spent a long time trying to put salt on their tails first so that they would not fly away. Much to her annoyance the salt never worked, despite the words and pictures on the Cerebos Salt packet, but her mother agreed that the birds were delighted to be free, and sometimes they would listen together and think they heard a bird chirping 'thank you' in Hindustani.

But the rabbits were different. They had to be kept in a cage because they would become a *plague* if they escaped. Rabbits bred very fast, her mother told her, and dug great holes in the earth called warrens and then you could never find them. Melanie thought that was a good idea for the rabbits: but her father said that they would overrun the whole country and eat all the food meant for people and the people already had very little food. In fact, her father said, you only had to look at a rabbit and it would have babies. Melanie spent a lot of time looking at her rabbits but they never had babies, much to her disappointment. Her mother said it would be a good thing if they didn't have babies because dogs liked eating rabbits and Kelly might eat the babies. Melanie didn't like the sound of that. She spent a long time 'training' Kelly to like her rabbits. Every evening when the sun was setting Melanie would let the rabbits out of their cage and she and Kelly would play with them, until Kelly became too boisterous and had to be shut away.

Melanie loved her rabbits passionately with their soft white fur, long pink ears and red eyes. Her mother said that the rabbits were called 'albinos' and had to be kept out of the sunlight or they would die. Melanie thought the rabbits were very silly to have been born in Pakistan because it was always very hot and sunny. Why had the rabbits been born in a country where they couldn't go out in the day? Her mother explained that the rabbits were specially bred to be eaten, but Melanie couldn't believe that anyone would *really* eat such pretty little creatures. It was a puzzlement: until she saw the rabbit in the kitchen.

At first she thought that Cook had killed one of her rabbits to eat — suddenly he seemed to her to be an ogre — but then she saw that the rabbit had blue eyes so she knew it wasn't one of hers. But she hated the cook after that. Besides, as she told her mother, her rabbits must either have seen the dead one in the kitchen or have heard about it in a special rabbit way, because afterwards they were never as happy and had no interest in playing with her and Kelly. In fact, they ran away and hid whenever Kelly came on to the balcony, her red tongue hanging out over her teeth as she panted, and flung herself down in the shade on the cool marble floor.

Almost before she knew it, Melanie found herself sitting next to her fragrant mother in the back of the car, while her father sat next to the driver in the front. Between his fingers glowed a lighted cigarette, but he was so busy speaking to the driver in Hindustani that he seldom put it to his lips. His arm rested on the sill of the open window, the white shirt sleeve rolled up to his elbow exposed his arm, so tanned it was almost black, and the sun glinted on the golden hairs on his skin and the silver band of his wristwatch.

As they drew out of the drive Melanie turned round to kneel on the leather seat and wave to the servants who all waved back, smiling. She would always remember them like that, smiling and waving.

Her mother made an odd little sound in her throat. Melanie recognised it as a sob and turned to her in consternation.

"Don't cry, Mummy. Look, they're all waving."

"I'm not crying, darling. I just have a frog in my throat."

Why did adults say such silly things? Melanie thought, as she put her arms around her mother. Obviously Mummy didn't have a frog in her throat! And just as obviously she was holding back tears. Why, she was even wearing her dark glasses which she never did unless she was trying to hide eyes red from weeping.

It had been the same when Granny died, although the

realisation then that her mother was crying real tears had come as something of a shock. Hadn't her mother told her that your tears dry up when you become an adult? Melanie had believed her because she never saw her cry when she hurt herself. Melanie had *tried* very hard to be brave when she shut her finger in the car door, but the tears had streamed down her cheeks nonetheless, and they did not stop falling even when her mother sang the lullaby 'O my darling, goodnight' that usually magicked her to sleep.

When Granny died, Daddy had come home early from work, in his hand a telegram and an airline ticket. Her mother had come downstairs from her afternoon sleep still in her pretty housecoat, the one with the appliquéd flowers on the bodice, and then he and Mummy had been hugging each other very tight and Mummy had asked her to go and find Kelly in a strangled sort of voice. And then her mother had cried real tears while she packed her suitcase and within an hour or two she had gone. Melanie remembered the pain in her chest when she saw her mother's tears and the feeling of desertion when the car had driven away to the airport. Her father had tried to explain that Mummy had had to go quickly because *her* mother was dying in England, but the hard black feeling had stayed in Melanie's heart.

Now, she could feel it beginning to spread all through her body, like a nameless dread, as she cuddled up to her mother, who blew her nose and smiled, saying that they had a very exciting journey ahead of them, but it would be good to look out of the window because it might be a long time before they came back to Karachi.

"When *will* we come back?" the little girl asked.

"Not for a year or two, darling. Perhaps not even then. We are going to India now — and you know what there are in India?"

"What?"

"Elephants!"

"Real, live elephants?"

"Yes, darling," her mother smiled fondly. "Real, huge, live elephants!"

"With trunks for noses?"

"With trunks for noses, and flappy ears ..."

"... and little eyes..."

"... and grey wrinkly skin ..."

"... and feet the size of ancient trees?"

"The very same, my darling girl!"

"And will Tim and Amy come and stay so I can show them the elephants?"

"Perhaps, darling. But look out of the window now and wave goodbye to Pakistan."

Melanie had been sorry to say goodbye to the servants. They had done their best to look after her when her mother had flown home to England, but her father had soon arranged for her to stay with her friends, Tim and Amy, who lived next door. Michael didn't count as a friend because he was only two and was always with his ayah, but Tim and Amy showed her how to climb the tree in their garden, and how to jump down from the verandah on to the dusty rose bed underneath. And when their parents were fast asleep, Tim and Amy had woken her up in the middle of the night and shown her how to creep downstairs and raid the fridge for a midnight feast.

Yes, Melanie had hated saying goodbye to Tim and Amy because she knew she would miss them most of all. But not Michael because he was just a baby, and rather annoying.

The car bumped down the short stretch of dirt road and turned left on to the newly tarmacked road that would take them into the centre of Karachi.

"What will happen to the servants now, Mummy?" Melanie asked softly. She didn't want the driver to hear, but the warm dusty draught coming in through the open windows was noisy enough to drown her words.

"They will find new employers, I'm sure. I think Mr Singh is going back to his village because his wife is sick, but we have recommended the others to the new Resident Engineer, Mr Black. Do you remember? He was at the party when Daddy retired."

Melanie remembered being the only child at a very dull party with nasty dry bits of food, watery orange squash for her (though the grown-ups were drinking alcohol and speaking far too loudly), long tedious speeches, a sort of flowery presentation followed by a formal photograph. The best part of the whole affair had been the garlands of flowers that had been presented to her parents. Her mother secretly took one string from hers and put it round her daughter's neck. Her father was busy, so apart from Mummy, the only person who had taken any notice of Melanie was her father's secretary, Mrs Watson.

Melanie thought she was lovely: very, very pretty with her dark hair and eyes and lightly tanned skin, but not nearly as pretty as Mummy, of course. Mrs Watson spoke very fast in a soft voice and Melanie was sure she was sad Daddy was leaving, because she smiled at him but when she looked at Mr Black her mouth turned down at the corners.

Her father shook hands with everybody and made that funny purring noise, half-cough half-laugh as if he was joking, but his eyes looked odd, all big and wet behind his glasses. Melanie thought that this was a bit peculiar, but it was all so boring that she went out into the garden and sat under the jacaranda tree where she took off her garland and tried to guess the names of all the threaded flowers. Melanie loved the blooms: their fragrance they made her head feel whirly and, when she pressed them against her cheek, their brilliantly coloured petals — of red, yellow, white, pink — felt as soft as Mummy's silk scarf. But the flowers' heads had been cut off from their stems so they couldn't drink and that made her sad.

When the last photographs had been taken and the last hands shaken, all three of them were driven home by the driver in the big black car with silver wheels. Melanie noticed that Mummy was sad behind her smile and Daddy's moustache drooped more than usual, but he clasped her hand in his big one and told her that she had behaved beautifully and he was very proud of her. Then he chuckled, chucked her under the chin and asked her what was black and white and red all over. So she said 'a newspaper' (which she knew was the right answer because it was a riddle and 'red' meant 'read') and knew he wouldn't be sad for long.

Her parents went straight to bed for a snooze and she was left to her own devices, so she had unstrung the garlands and put the flower heads in a bowl of water. But the flowers still couldn't drink because they only had heads and no stems, so by the morning they were brown and dead and smelled unpleasant. How could people be so cruel to flowers?

Yes, she remembered Mr Black. He was a severe-looking man who was rude to Mrs Watson and he had been given a garland, too. She threw caution to the winds and frowned.

"I remember Mr Black," Melanie said. "I didn't like him. He was rude to Mrs Watson."

"I don't think he meant to be, darling."

"Yes, he did! He said she was 'of a class'. That sounds rude. And it made her cry."

"I think he only meant that she was Anglo-Indian."

"What's Anglo-indian?"

"It means that she has one English parent and one Indian parent."

"But that's good, isn't it?"

"Yes, I think so."

"Well, I like Mrs Watson. And I don't like Mr Black. Is he going to live in our house?"

"Probably. Melanie, look! There's a bullock cart ahead. Shall we overtake it?"

Melanie shrugged. "We always do."

"And there are camels, and a donkey cart."

"But no elephants."

Her mother smiled. "No, but we will see elephants in Bombay, I promise."

"I know where we are now," Melanie observed as the smell of the river invaded the car. The occupants hurriedly wound up the windows to shut out the stench caused by too many bodies in one place without any sanitation. "We're by the refugee camp."

A couple of little boys were running along the side of the road trying to keep up with the car. They were wearing only a top garment, a shirt of some sort, and, not having any little brothers herself, Melanie was fascinated by their bare genitals. She knew better than to say so, but the sight of them bobbing up and down made her giggle and hide her face in her hands.

"Baksheesh! baksheesh! No whisky, no soda, no mama, no papa," they chanted as they ran, rubbing their tummies in circular fashion. The car had slowed behind the bullock cart which was taking up most of the road and proceeding at walking pace, so the children were able to keep up. The tallest suddenly stuck out his tongue. Melanie replied by sticking hers out too. Luckily the boys were running close by the window on her side of the car so Mummy didn't realise she was being so rude. The boys giggled, put their thumbs in their ears

26

and wiggled their fingers at her. She couldn't do that because her mother would see, but she wiggled her nose instead. Like a rabbit, she thought.

"Here, give them this." Melanie's mother gave her a handful of silver annas. Melanie quickly wound down the window and threw out the money — just in time, because a gap in the oncoming traffic had provided the driver with an opportunity to overtake the cart. The car swung out and accelerated. The children scrabbled to pick up the money and were lost from view. Mummy leant over and rapidly wound up the window but not before the stink had permeated the car.

Melanie remembered asking her father why the river always smelled so bad. He had explained that people could live without much food but they needed water to stay alive, to drink and wash and keep clean.

"But water doesn't smell," she'd complained.

"Not when it comes out of the tap," he'd agreed. "But when it's mixed with mud in the river, it's a bit more pongy. Especially when you have lots of people living in one place without a lavatory, it stinks."

"But why…?"

"I'll tell you a story," he'd interrupted. "A true story, and a very sad one, so listen carefully."

She had kept very quiet and listened as carefully as she knew how. And he had explained that, After-The-War (every piece of information was always preceded by the words 'after-the-war', 'during-the-war', 'before-the-war' or 'before-you-were-born') and around the time she was born in 1947, India had finally decided that it had had enough of the British Raj and wanted to be an independent country.

"But why?" she'd interrupted.

Daddy had sighed, taken off his glasses and polished them on his handkerchief. She liked it when she could see his eyes properly. They were a browny-green and very big, but his eyelashes had been worn down by his lenses and there was a deep mark on the bridge of his nose where the spectacles customarily sat.

"India is a wonderful country," he said. "But because it has always been rich and full of jewels and treasure that other people wanted, it has suffered from wars all through the centuries. It is made up of lots of states that used to be separate countries, until the British came along and combined them all into one."

"Yes, that was called the British Raj," the little girl nodded. "And it was a good thing, wasn't it?"

Daddy replaced his spectacles: the lenses reflected the light so she couldn't see his eyes any more. "I expect you have been told so. And yes, it was, in some ways. The British brought their ways of running a country with them and for a long time there was peace and justice and the trains ran on time and everything went swimmingly. No-one could come to India and not be changed by it, and many people made their fortunes and went 'home' to England, only to find the country cold, wet and tedious. So they would come back to India and sometimes they married Indian ladies and stayed here. But the English were few and thought themselves much more special than they really were. And eventually the Indians had enough of being bossed about."

"But you boss the Pakistanis about, Daddy!"

Daddy smiled ruefully and patted her shoulder. "Yes, but they work for me, sweetheart. That's different."

"And Mummy bossed the driver's wife about when she told her she could only live in the garage if she came out of purdah!"

"Mummy was helping the driver's wife, darling. Remember it was Mummy who gave them the garage to live in when their hut was washed away in the monsoon? And Mummy didn't insist about the driver's wife coming out of purdah when she saw how troubled she was about not wearing a veil in public."

"But she was still *bossy* — and so are you!"

Daddy chuckled. "Yes, you're right, darling! So you see why the Indians got fed up with the British and in the end threw them out of the country."

"But it's all right in Pakistan isn't it? Because we're here. And you're still bossing people about."

"All right, darling, I'll admit it! I *am* bossy. But the British don't govern either India or Pakistan any more. Each country has its own parliament and its own president."

Melanie found this statement very puzzling, but she wasn't sure what to say so she resorted to sucking her thumb while her father continued: "You see, India and Pakistan used to be one big country called India, but when the British left it was decided to make two new separate countries out of the old one. That is the sad part, because for centuries people of all religions and cultures lived side by side in India quite happily — or at least without major disputes — but when India was granted independence it somehow happened that the Muslims and Hindus wanted separate states, and that was what was finally agreed. So Pakistan was formed for the Muslims because there was a majority of them in this area of the Punjab. But that led to a huge problem. The Hindus in Pakistan wanted to move to India and the Muslims in India wanted to come to Pakistan. Hundreds of thousands of people packed up all the belongings they could carry and walked to the other country. They were seeking refuge so they were called 'refugees'."

Melanie took her thumb out of her mouth long enough to say: "But that doesn't explain why it's so smelly, Daddy!"

Her father grinned. "No, it doesn't! You're right again. This is the reason for that: the people who came here to Pakistan came with nothing other than the clothes they were wearing and a few, *very* few, possessions. When they arrived here they had nowhere to live, no job, no livelihood, no food. They just camped where they could. They came to the city to find work, but there was nowhere to live so they just patched together a shack. And, as you know, lots of families are squashed into a tiny little living space. They needed water so they camped close to the river. "

Her father paused and looked out of the window. The little girl looked up, her attention captured by his sudden silence.

"Many of these refugees are proud gracious people

who have been reduced to a life in the refugee camp by circumstances beyond their control," he said.

It seemed to Melanie, then, that her father was talking more to himself than to her, but after a few moments he continued: "Soon more and more people were flooding in, and all of them had to drink and wash and relieve themselves. With so many people tramping to the river, the banks were trodden into mud. All these desperate people are living in very unhygienic conditions — and that makes the place stink to high heaven, especially in the hot season when the river is low and the sun is hot."

Melanie nodded, still sucking her thumb. 'Unhygienic', Daddy had said. That explained a lot. Mummy was always very careful to make sure that things were hygienic so that they did not get ill. She insisted Melanie flushed the toilet after she had 'been'; that she bathed each night before bed and always washed her hands before she ate. It was to make sure that she didn't get ill or get worms in her stomach.

"Do the refugees get ill, then, Daddy?"

Her father started at this sudden question. "Yes. As a matter of fact, they do. Horrible illnesses, born of starvation, squalor, bad water and flies. And many die."

"It's very, very sad," the little girl said, feeling the weight of her father's thoughts.

"Yes, it is. And the worst of it is that it's all because of the stupidity of humans."

But Melanie was thinking of the driver and of how, even when he was living in the refugee camp with his wife and three little children, he always looked bandbox clean and smart when he came to work; and how he hadn't died and nor had his wife who was so pretty or his children who were so tiny and sweet. She said as much to her father.

"Yes, it's a miracle," he replied.

Melanie decided to pray for a lot more miracles, little realising that a good deal of this 'miracle' had been her mother's doing when she had rescued the family from the refugee camp by the river.

Perhaps Jesus, who, the Bible said, had changed water into wine, could make wine into pure clear water? Daddy kept a lot of wine in the fridge, she thought. Maybe that would be a good place to start.

- 4 -

Bombay, India 1954

Bom-bay. Bombay. Melanie loved the sound of the word and the feel of it in her mouth. As she played with her dolls on the deck of the ship carrying them from Pakistan, she kept saying over and over:

"Drink up your tea, Matilda! We're going to Bombay ... Bombay ... Bombay. We're going to Bombay ... Bombay ... Bombay."

The words became a song which she taught to her dolls. She knew they loved the name and the song because they always smiled and ate up their tiny sandwiches — though sometimes she had to help them because their eyes were bigger than their bellies, as Mummy would say. Melanie noticed that the sound of Matilda's 'maa-ma' — the noise she made when Melanie turned her over to change her nappy — altered from a lament to excitement. Sometimes Melanie thought the lessons she gave Matilda in how to speak were beginning to have effect. Matilda could never say 'Karachi' but sometimes the ma-ma word sounded a little like 'bom-ba'.

"Listen," she would say to her mother. "Matilda's growing up. She can say 'Bom-ba' now!"

Melanie knew that her mother's fond smile was for her and not for Matilda's cleverness, but that didn't matter a jot because she knew exactly what her doll was feeling — Matilda was looking forward to her new home as much as Melanie was herself.

The ship followed the Indian shoreline, a thin smudge of blue-grey mist ever-present on the port side of the boat. In the evening a light sometimes sparkled from the shore. Her father said the flashes came from a lighthouse that had been built to warn ships that there were rocks in the sea. Then he would take her up to the wheelhouse to watch the helmsman turn the huge ship's wheel and they would feel the change in the vibration of the planks under their feet and a different sound from the engine.

Afterwards, her father would take her down to the stern of the boat and hold her high up so that she was standing on the ship's rail, with his arm about her to steady her. Together they would watch the plunging rudder weaving a wavy trail of white water pluming in the ship's wake and he would tell her that if the rudder went to the left the boat would steer to the right and vice versa. Sometimes, when they watched by moonlight or starlight, the phosphorous in the boat's trail would spark red, green and blue on the surface of the water. At other times, in the daylight, they would see flying fish. Great shoals of them would leap high into the air together like the corps-de-ballet she had seen when her mother had taken her to see Les Sylphides at Covent Garden in London, a long time ago when she was a very little girl of only four years of age.

One day, when she was on deck with her father she saw a huge silver fish jump out of the water and flip right round in the air.

"Look!" she yelled, tugging on her father's hand — but he was deep in conversation with one of the crew in a language she did not understand and he took no notice of her. Another fish jumped, or perhaps it might have been the same one. "Look! Daddy, look!" she shouted, bouncing up and down with excitement — and this time he did turn round.

"Porpoises!" he cried. "Where's Mummy? We must tell her, Melanie."

But, from where she was half-reading, half-dreaming in the steamer chair on the after deck, Melanie's mother had already heard her daughter's joyous shout. She hurriedly put down the book and joined them at the ship's rail, and soon all of them were smiling and laughing at an amazing display of acrobatics by a team of aquatic athletes. The fish seemed to be teasing the humans, playing with them, showing off, wanting to make them happy.

The porpoises followed the boat for two days. Every now and again, apparently from sheer joy, they would leap clear of the water; sometimes they came so close to the ship that Melanie could see their shining eyes and their chuckling faces; sometimes there was only one fish, sometimes two or three would skim along beside the boat in unison; and on one marvellous occasion shortly before they reached Bombay, a whole pod of some twenty creatures put on a stunning display. After that they disappeared from view and were not seen again.

Melanie would have been sad had she known that

she would not see the porpoises again, but that very day the boat sailed into Bombay Harbour. Her father had promised Bombay was a beautiful city, called the 'Gateway to India'. And when the ship sailed into the harbour he took her on deck to watch as it docked. The sun glittered on the sea and Melanie had to screw up her eyes to see anything at all — even though they had been at sea for a few days now and she was used to watching the waves sparkle in the sunlight. Somehow it was different here, as if the sun were brighter.

Ahead of them stretched a magnificent panorama. The sapphire sea filled the wide deep bay of the natural harbour, framed by the lush green of the mountains on the mainland. The harbour itself was studded with islands, like precious stones of emerald and jasper in a sea of liquid lapis lazuli, a shimmering deep blue flecked with gold and dotted with white diamonds — the sails of innumerable small craft skipping across the sea's sparkling surface. Hypnotised by its beauty, Melanie gazed upon its splendour with silent unalloyed delight.

Her father laughed and said, pointing with his finger: "Look there, sweetheart. The Gateway to India."

To their right rose a huge, impressive archway. Constructed of sand-coloured basalt right on the waterline, it reared to a height of more than ninety feet, and the whole of the surface was intricately carved and patterned. From its foot, short jetties jutted out into the harbour. Boats of all sizes were moored to three of them, a large sleek craft was moored to a fourth and the fifth was completely empty. Melanie wondered what it would be like to land there with the great building soaring skywards so close, and felt daunted at the prospect.

"See the empty jetty, there, sweetheart? That's only used for ceremonial occasions now. In the old days, when the Viceroy of India ..."

"Who's the Viceroy of India?" his daughter interrupted, frowning.

"Do you remember that I told you the British ruled India?"

"Yes, before I was born."

"That's right! Well, the Viceroy used to be appointed by the King to represent him in India — so he was treated as if he were the King, with all the same ceremonies."

The little girl's brow cleared. "Was he allowed to go through the Gateway?"

Her father laughed and, ruffling the little girl's curls, said: "Precisely! When he took his first steps ashore from the ship that had brought him here — all the way from England — he would enter India through that imposing gateway."

The Gateway was beginning to slide out of their line of vision and they both leaned forward to keep it in view for as long as possible.

"But did the King and Queen ever go through it, Daddy?"

Her father looked thoughtful. "I don't think so. I know it was built to *commemorate* the landing in Bombay of King George V and Queen Mary when they made a state visit to India in 1911 — long before you were born — but it wasn't finished until 1924."

"That was before I was born, too!" Melanie looked quite triumphant about making this deduction.

Her father changed the subject.

"Look there's the island called Elephanta. It's famous for the huge statue of an elephant that stood there by the sea."

"I can't see the elephant."

"No, it fell in the sea when the Portuguese tried to take it away." Melanie's face fell. "But they found it and moved it on to dry land. I'll take you to see it when we've had a chance to unpack."

Melanie never forgot that first sight of Bombay from the harbour, and sixty years later it is still the first image she sees behind her eyelids when India is mentioned. Instantly, almost before the image forms, the smell of the subcontinent is in her nostrils. How can she describe India's special fragrance? A fragrance like a spiritual blessing — an intuition others might say — an impression formed on the sensibilities of a child that never leaves her, but becomes the memory of the place itself.

So Melanie's memories are compounded of smiles; white, white teeth in dark faces illuminated by dark liquid eyes; noses studded with gold; gold armbands and bracelets; the light, bright colours of saris; check Madras shirts; bicycles, scooters, buses; people everywhere; loaded in lorries, buses, trains, hanging out of windows, from cars and scooters; red betel gum spattering the streets; the compound unnameable smell — of cigarettes, petrol fumes, excrement, spices and incense mixed with the faint scent of greenery; and noise, noise, noise.

And then, something else intervenes ... slowing the pulse, calming her heartbeat, curving her lips in a smile of remembrance. Elephants. Their slow lumbering ungainly gait; strange long appendages for noses; tiny eyes; huge mouths and great tongues; huge legs and round flat feet the size of ancient tree stumps; and a smell of the forest and a longing for the forest; a jangling of chains ... and sorrow. Sorrow so great that it bears heavily on the atmosphere; a yearning for freedom so immense that it hangs upon the heart like a miasma, never to be shifted; and yet there is humour there too, and a sense of mischief; gentleness and a knowing that goes deep, deep, and deeper still; deeper than words, deeper than the moment; deeper than the heart's ancient knowing; a strange consciousness of the primeval world; a wisdom dating back into the mists of time when all was One.

- 5 -

Lakshmi

Melanie did not want an ayah.

She did not need an ayah. She was six-and-three-quarters years of age — far too old for a nursemaid. Besides she had Mummy. She had not had a nursemaid, or an ayah, ever! And she did not need one now. She was, she thought, managing perfectly well without one.

Unusually for her, because she was generally a very biddable little girl, she stamped her foot in rage and ran off into the gardens, there to hide inside the rhododendron bush where she had made a nest for herself. None of the other children knew of her camp; they had ayahs who never let them do anything exciting.

How she didn't want an ayah! She burst into tears of frustration. In truth, they were tears of worry, sadness and fear as well as frustration, because she knew that, had her mother been in good health, she would not even be considering appointing an ayah to look after her daughter.

Melanie could read the signs now. She knew that her mother in a great deal of pain. She noticed the spasms that crossed her face and the sheen of sweat that glowed on her brow, although her mother always smiled afterwards and said it was nothing, just the weather or something she had eaten that had 'disagreed' with her. There was nothing for Melanie to worry about.

But Melanie did worry: she noticed that her lovely warm, vibrant mother was beginning to look like the flowers in the garland, beautiful and fragrant but slowly wilting, slowly dying. She stopped the thought in its tracks. Mummy would have told her if she were seriously ill, surely? Or if Mummy didn't, surely Daddy would tell her? Perhaps it was just a stomach pain after all. But then, Melanie knew that her mother couldn't sleep, that most nights she slept in a bath of cold water, right through until morning.

"It's so comfortable, darling," her mother would say. But Melanie knew that to lie in a hard bath all night would not be at all comfortable, even with the little cushion on which her mother pillowed her head.

So perhaps she ought to be good and kind like Jesus and agree to Mummy's suggestion. Melanie supposed it would not be too bad to have someone to take you for walks, or to parties, or to meet you from school. In her heart of hearts, she knew that her mother simply could not walk far, even though she tried to disguise this fact from her daughter. Perhaps looking after Melanie was making her worse, maybe she needed to lie on the sofa all day like the invalids did in the olden days, and then she would get better.

Melanie crawled out from her hiding place, dusted down her grubby knees, pulled her full skirt out from the knicker legs where she'd tucked it up for ease of movement, and smoothed it down. She crept back into the flat and into the bathroom where she washed her hands and face, not entirely successfully, brushed the twigs out of her hair and stole softly into the sitting room. Her mother was resting on the sofa, her eyes closed. For once, her face was peaceful.

"There you are, darling," she said without opening her eyes. "I knew you would come back in a little while. How is your den in the rhododendrons?"

Melanie gasped. How did her mother know?

"The gardener told me," Mummy answered the unspoken thought, opening her eyes slowly and smiling. "I'm so glad. Every little girl should have a special place. I used to climb trees. Just be careful of snakes and spiders."

Melanie took a deep breath. It was now or never. Now, while she was feeling brave.

"I *will* have an ayah, Mummy, if you really want me to."

Mrs Elizabeth Russell sat on the sofa with her feet on a footstool and interviewed a string of potential ayahs, which was not such an easy process as it might at first seem. She sighed. It was one thing to decide that Melanie needed an ayah, quite another to find one who was suitable.

First of all, there was Melanie to consider. She needed a light hand on the reins, someone she could trust and someone who could be trusted to look after her. And if they could learn to love each other, so much the better.

Then there were the other servants: it was not easy to find a servant one could trust, let alone one who would get on with the other staff. If and when one did, one had to make sure it was clearly understood that bullying or other political jockeying for standing or favour would not be tolerated. And yet, she owed her employees a great deal. Between them they had helped her by taking the brunt of caring for her little daughter while she herself was incapacitated. She shrugged, dismissing that problem for a moment: she would take care the Bearer approved her choice before she made the final appointment.

Next there was her husband, Harold, who was busy completing this latest civil engineering posting in the Indian sub-continent and who was somewhat irritable about the way he had been treated by the company — as if he were ready for retirement at only fifty-five. He had never been quite the same since the Japanese had invaded Burma and destroyed his comfortable life there. He had been forced to walk out of the country, stripped of all possessions but the clothes he was wearing: a refugee not unlike those who littered the banks of Karachi's great river. And no wonder! He had seen too much of death and disease in those months; when, starving, soaked through to the skin, ill, exhausted and shoeless he had trekked through the jungled hills of Burma in the downpour of the monsoon rains. Posted as missing, believed dead, she had thought him lost to her for ever, and indeed he was close to death when he reached the mission in Northern India. He had been confined there for several months more, suffering from jungle sores, malaria, dysentery and other less physical conditions.

They had lost everything in the War, everything but each other — and they were both changed, altered almost beyond recognition by the horrors they had seen and endured, for she had suffered too, albeit differently from him. His moods were erratic and he suffered from depression. Worse, he was now worried about her health. She dared not tell him what the doctor had intimated to her. Should her present illness prove to be her last, he would need someone on whom he could rely.

He loved Trevor, of course, but Melanie was his joy. Born after the War as a promise to the future, she had helped to re-cement their marriage, but she was so much more than that — she was lightness, happiness, thoughtfulness, hope and the future. Yes, she and Trevor were the future.

Elizabeth found herself day dreaming, remembering the halcyon days when Trevor was a baby. The life they had led in Burma had been exciting and comfortable, before the War had parted them from Harold. She missed her son greatly: they had been through so many terrifying times together. His safety and happiness had been all she could think about as they found themselves adrift in a lifeboat, watching the ship sink ….

She gave herself a mental shake — that had been a long time ago and had nothing to do with her present predicament. Anyway, she had eventually found a way to bring him safely home to England and now Trevor was nineteen and at university. Soon he would be a qualified veterinary surgeon. He was grown up and independent, but Melanie was just a child — a child whose mother was seriously ill.

For Melanie's sake, Elizabeth had to think of herself. She knew she needed time and rest to heal. Her body felt worn out and painful: she was feverish, could hardly eat and the pain in her bowels gnawed at her sanity, so that the only respite she could find was by soaking in a bath full of cold water. Perhaps all these symptoms would improve after the operation, but the doctor had warned that she would require 'proper nursing' and bed rest for at least three months after she came home from hospital.

Although she had drawn on all the strength she possessed to interview a line of prospective ayahs, none of them had seemed right. One was too strict, another too young, a third was too arrogant, a fourth too confident of her beauty — she would cause rifts in the household for certain! The fifth, an old woman with a sad story, bent and wrinkled and for whom her heart bled, would have found Melanie too lively. Instead, she gave the woman a handful of rupees and decided to tell her husband a small fib about the expense. He denied her nothing, but he feared that too much generosity would encourage theft should word of it spread amongst the locals.

Having interviewed five women, she now felt wrung out, exhausted. She needed someone to take care of Melanie, and she needed that person immediately. Sighing, she closed her eyes in prayer and sent an urgent, fervent supplication to the Almighty.

There came the Bearer's light knock on the door, and the soft click as it opened. She heard the swish of a sari and the padding of bare feet, smelled the rather strong perfume that the Bearer favoured and behind it something else. A faint aroma compounded of a little curry, a little perfume and the patchouli-cardamon scent of a sari kept for special occasions. Her intuition detected something more, which she found difficult to categorise, something that indicated to her that she was in the presence of female goodness and maturity.

She opened her eyes. Before her, to one side, stood the Bearer, and beside and slightly behind him, a substantial Indian woman swathed in a pink sari edged with gold, which covered her down-bent head.

The Bearer bowed, his hands steepled together at his chest in the greeting of the East.

"Memsahib," he said softly with the musical inflection of the Hindi speaker. "With the utmost greatest of respect from the very-most bottom of my heart, may I present to you my aunt? She is the very-most experienced of women for most genuinely attending and, I may say, disciplining, with young-small children, but is now thrown upon hard times. Having been until utmost recently employed as an ayah to the English family with five of the smallest persons, she would still be most solicitously disciplining of them had it not been for the most utmost miserable misfortune that the father of the family has been posted back to England. But, alas! She is now most poor and even, I would say, destitute. And having no other family of her own, she is come to me to beg for me to find her employment. Which I now do, Memsahib, with the greatest humility and respect."

When he had finished speaking, the Bearer bowed

again and stepped back, firmly indicating to his companion that she should step forward. Again the soft swish of the sari and that faint scent.

Despite her exhaustion and physical discomfort, Elizabeth experienced considerable difficulty in keeping a straight face while she listened in silence to this flowery speech. Hiding her smile behind her hand she managed, with great effort, to school her features into seriousness. She thanked the Bearer calmly and indicated that he should leave the room. She very much doubted that the woman was, in truth, his aunt, but she greatly respected the Indian sense of responsibility for their extended family. She also knew that it was unlikely that the woman would respond to her questions with anything other than monosyllables while the Bearer was present.

The Bearer bowed again and exited the room on silent slippered feet, leaving the two women alone. Elizabeth relaxed and allowed herself to smile at the latest applicant for the job: the woman beamed back, her smile lighting up the room as well as her rather plain features. Her teeth were large, crooked and stained with betel but their imperfection somehow added to her natural charm. The smile crinkled the corners of her eyes and spread her large nose, decorated with a proportionately-sized nose ring, across her wide dark face. Despite her plainness, the smile showed the middle-aged woman's special beauty, demonstrating better than words the grace of maturity, kindness and understanding. And her eyes were kind beyond measure.

She put her hands together and bowed her head.

With her smile hidden it seemed the light in the room dimmed.

"Namaste, Memsahib."

Elizabeth returned the gesture and invited the woman to sit on a chair close by.

"Please tell me your name?"

"Lakshmi, Memsahib."

"Your nephew certainly recommends you for this post. Has he mentioned that you would only be required to attend to one little girl? Her name is Melanie and she is six years old."

"Yes, mem," Lakshmi said seriously and then lapsed into giggles.

Looking back, Elizabeth realised that it was Lakshmi's giggles that had decided her, although she led Lakshmi through the appropriate questions before she informed her that the ayah's position was hers. It was helpful that she had been recommended by the Bearer, for that meant Elizabeth did not have to worry herself about Lakshmi's acceptance by the staff.

The Englishwoman had no doubt that Life had not dealt kindly with Lakshmi, yet it was clear from her bearing that Lakshmi had dealt gently and selflessly with Life.

Sending Lakshmi into the kitchen, she instructed her to inform the Bearer that she had been employed and that he must make sure she was provided with a meal .

Having made the decision, Elizabeth felt as though a great weight had been lifted from her, and sent a quick prayer of gratitude aloft. She had found Melanie an ayah she deserved, and perhaps Lakshmi deserved a kind well-behaved little girl like Melanie as her charge.

Melanie's father collected her from school the day that Lakshmi was appointed — an unusual but happy occurrence because her father always worked so hard that he was seldom home before Melanie went to bed.

"I have a surprise for you," he said. Melanie tried to guess what the surprise was, but to no avail: none of her guesses was right. Her father chuckled as he lit another cigarette. "You'll see when we get home."

Although her wide clear brow showed only patience, Lakshmi was waiting in some apprehension to meet her latest charge. She was getting too old for this, she thought: she was nearing sixty and had grown heavier as she aged. She noticed the change in the seasons these days and her bones ached, especially her knees. She could no longer run after recalcitrant children without getting severely breathless, or play the games that the young ayahs enjoyed with their charges. Sometimes she wondered if she were dying, not that the thought of death worried her. No, what concerned her was that she had no-one to care for her when she could no longer work. She had no husband, no children, her parents had died long since and her brothers and sisters had all perished when she was a child, in one of the epidemics that raged across the country each year after the monsoon rains.

She had hoped to stay with the English family she

had just left — five children of assorted ages, the youngest a babe-in-arms. She had felt settled, if not happy, with that family, knowing that they would need the services of an ayah for several years — perhaps even long enough for her to save a little money, so that she would not be a problem for anyone. If she could only pay her way....

She sighed so softly it was scarcely noticeable: her cousin's sister-in-law's nephew had been good to speak on her behalf, and she was grateful. But what would happen at the end of this employment when she was another eight months older? The new memsahib had warned her that the family would be taking ship in a few months time to return to England and so could not offer her a permanent post.

"Here you are, sweetheart. This is Lakshmi, your ayah. Lakshmi, this is my daughter, Melanie."

The little girl ran into the room, only to stop dead, her disappointment showing in her face, when she saw Lakshmi. Melanie was dismayed with her surprise: she didn't think an ayah was a proper surprise at all! She glanced over her shoulder at her father. Immediately judging that this was not the moment to complain, she hung her head and resorted to sucking her thumb. Lakshmi knew better than to make any move towards the child — she must come to her in her own time — so she stayed immobile and allowed herself to be scrutinised by a pair of honest green eyes.

Melanie's father was becoming impatient. "Now, sweetheart, you know it's rude to stare. Shake hands

with Lakshmi and say 'how-do-you-do' properly."
The little girl took her thumb out of her mouth, wiped
it on her skirt and held out her hand to her ayah. "How
do you do, Lakshmi?"
Lakshmi's face broke into a genuine smile and
Melanie found herself smiling back. "Very well, very well
indeed, Missy! And may I ask how you are doing
yourself?" She took the little hand in hers but did not let
go.
Melanie had never been asked the formal
introductory question in quite the same way. In fact, no-
one usually bothered to answer her at all. A smile or a
perfunctory nod was usually deemed sufficient
acknowledgement for a child in situations where a formal
greeting was expected.
Melanie decided that Lakshmi was very nice, even if
she did smell different from Mummy. Of course, she was
so *old*, and tubby too, like Daddy — but then he was very
old too, much older than everyone else's father. All the
children thought he was her grandpa — which was silly
— just because he was bald with a little grey hair round
the edges. Grandpas were tall and thin with white hair
parted at the side, long wide noses and twinkly brown
eyes. She knew *that*! Because she had a grandpa in
England like everyone else. No-body in India had a
grandpa, unless they were Indian.
Melanie was sorry that she had frowned at Lakshmi,
who was wearing a beautiful sari in her favourite colour,
bright pink, and it even had gold edging.
"I like your sari, Lakshmi," she said and didn't stop

talking. Lakshmi squatted beside the little girl as she rattled off a full account of the events of her day in school, including the fact that her father had collected her, which was most unusual, and had promised her a surprise when she got home — not that she thought an ayah was a *surprise* — but she did like her nose ring and the rings on her toes. Did it hurt to go around all day in bare feet? Mummy wouldn't let her in case she got worms but she hated shoes, and especially socks, because they were so hot! And she was very hungry and what was there for tea? And afterwards could they go for a walk *please*, because Mummy had said that when she had an ayah she could go for a walk in the Hanging Gardens and her friend Linda at school had said there was a big boot in the gardens for children to play in? Mummy couldn't take her, you see, because she wasn't well and couldn't walk far.

The child's eyes clouded over and she squeezed the hand she was still holding. "Do you think Mummy's going to die, Lakshmi?" A tear leaked out of the corner of her left eye. "I'm so worried."

Again she glanced over her shoulder, suddenly remembering that her father was there — and Mummy had made her promise not to say anything to Daddy about Mummy not being well enough to walk, because Daddy would only worry and that wouldn't help, it would just make him sad. But once he had seen Melanie chattering away to Lakshmi as if she had known the Indian woman all her short life, her father had left the room, quietly closing the door behind him. They were alone, the old Indian woman and the little English girl, but they were together, the bond between them unspoken but strong, as if they had been together before. Perhaps in another life, Lakshmi thought.

"English ladies need rest to be well, Missy. Your mummy will be resting while you are playing and that will be very good indeed for her! And if you are playing that will be very good indeed for you! And it will make your mother very happy, too. And if you are both being very good and also being very happy then you will both be as well as you can be."

Melanie put her arms round Lakshmi's neck and said seriously: "I have known you, before." But the next moment she had pulled away and was tugging at Lakshmi's hand, as the elderly woman struggled a little to straighten her knees.

"Tea! Tea! Please, Lakshmi, I'm so hungry!"

"Yes! Yes indeed, Missy! But first you must go and see your mother. And you must tell her that you will be a good girl for your poor old Lakshmi."

Afterwards, Elizabeth wondered how she would ever have coped had it not been for Lakshmi. She had been so ill since before they arrived in Bombay. The miscarriages, the surgical operations, the bowel problem, all had taken their toll on her health, and for months it seemed that the most she could do was move listlessly from sofa to bed and back again. And there was so much that she had wanted to do, so much to see and experience.

It was not in her nature to be an invalid. She was the

tomboy amongst her sisters, the one who led the jaunts into the woods, who climbed trees and skinned her knees, who ran wild in the country and came home grubby and exhausted. She was the one who was always reprimanded, who would never act like the lady she was expected to be, and whom, it was prophesied, no man would ever marry.

In the end she had been banished to an English boarding school for young ladies, where she was so unhappy that she ran away. She was soon found, of course, and punished by being gated, but that had not affected her independent streak. Circumstances changed considerably when the depression of the 1930s impoverished her family. She was forced to consider a career other than marriage.

Fortunately, she was granted a scholarship to learn, and ultimately teach, dance. Living with her aunt in London – to whom she had been sent to be 'finished' – she took several part-time jobs to finance her training. She had recently passed the teaching examinations when she met and enchanted Harold, a Civil Engineer in the Indian Civil Service. He was a good many years older than she and 'home' on leave for two months from his post in Burma. Before his leave was up they were engaged and within another month she was aboard a ship en route to Burma where she would marry him.

But within a few years, the Second World War had destroyed their life in Burma, and with it, her physical health and his sense of humour.

In Bombay, Harold found it difficult to relax, partly

because of the temporary nature of the post to which he had been appointed, although his anxiety about his wife's frail health was another strain on his meagre mental resources. Consequently he constantly over-worked and worried about his responsibilities, both business and personal. Elizabeth needed her own limited reserves to support him.

Melanie had always been her main charge, but Elizabeth also ran the whole household. This included overseeing the servants, resolving their petty squabbles, choosing the daily menu, organising the obligatory dinner parties, and ensuring all was perfect when her husband came home. People at home never understood that these were challenging tasks, especially when one was ill.

How lucky it was that she had not employed the pretty woman named Parva who had applied to be Melanie's ayah! She had been tempted, thinking that Melanie needed someone young to keep up with her and bring some liveliness into her life, but Parva had turned out to be a woman of dubious morals and young men were constantly coming and going through her bedroom window! Not at all what she would have wanted for Melanie.

No, without Lakshmi, she would never have coped. All her life, she would owe Lakshmi a debt. Elizabeth determined that Lakshmi would be handsomely recompensed when, in a few months time, the family left India for good.

Lakshmi was the only ayah that Melanie ever had,

while Lakshmi's whole life had consisted of caring for other people's children, children of another race with different values and aspirations. Elizabeth realised that, while Melanie was of an age to remember Lakshmi, the ayah's memory of Melanie — one small girl, whom she mothered for a little short of eight months — was likely to merge into her memories of all the other children she had nannied.

The Englishwoman would do her best to ensure that Lakshmi had other employment when the time came: there was nothing more she could do to protect her future.

Melanie had taken a while to settle in to her new school and was still not happy there. She was generally a gregarious little girl and she had loved the Grammar School she had attended in Karachi, but the move and her mother's illness had unsettled her. The Grammar School had been restricted to children of British officials working in government departments, but the Bombay school was larger. With more pupils, many of different nationalities, it was much more international in flavour; and to Melanie the children seemed much noisier and more physical than her Karachi classmates.

The only child she was comfortable with was Linda, the daughter of one of her father's colleagues, who was a year older and in a different class. Linda was learning the local language and Indian script, but Melanie was excused from these lessons because she and her parents would be leaving the country within a few months. Not only would Melanie have liked to learn how to read and write in the most common of the Indian languages, but her exclusion from those lessons meant that she finished school, on some days, an hour earlier than her schoolfellows, with the consequence that she was considered different and an outsider.

Half an hour before the pupils were ready to come home, their ayahs would gather and chatter outside the school gates in an unofficial club, useful for exchanging information and gossip as well as for fostering mutual support. Apart from this being a social meeting, it gave them a chance to discuss their charges' problems and difficulties, and to seek experienced help with them.

Thus Lakshmi learned that Melanie, bright and apparently happy outside school, was a reserved little mouse in the classroom. Seldom speaking to the other children or answering the teacher's questions, she preferred to suck her thumb and twist a lock of her hair.

Melanie knew that she would never fit in to this school. The other children teased her and the more they teased her, the more withdrawn she became; their noise and unruliness frankly scared her so much that she was frightened of joining in their games. She wasn't welcome anyway. She hated the big bullying boys with loud voices who pushed and squabbled and laughed at her, and the spoiled girls who accused her of being a boy because her hair was short. They would laugh and say that girls were not allowed to play with boys.

When her mother told her that she must play with the other children, she acquiesced, but when it came to it she was too shy. Besides, they all had friends already and no-one wanted to play with her. She sometimes played with Alan and Derek outside her father's Club, but they didn't attend her school. No one else was inclined to tolerate her. When her mother was watching, she pretended she was playing with some of the other children and managed to convince her that she was happy. In reality, she played on the periphery of the group and, more often than not, headed for her den in the rhododendrons where she could play undisturbed with her dolls.

Of course, when Lakshmi — well-experienced in the ways of children, particularly white, privileged and snobbish ones, — came into Melanie's life, the little girl could not pull the wool over her ayah's eyes.

Lakshmi felt a kinship with the little girl without siblings, adrift in a sea of adults who were themselves ill and busy with little time for the child. Recognising that the little girl was gradually becoming more and more withdrawn, she determined to find some way to help her.

Melanie talked constantly of Kelly the dog, the birds she had bought to set free so they could fly away, Cook's bantam hens and her beloved white rabbits; but pets were not allowed in the flat her parents were renting.

While Lakshmi was chatting with the other ayahs, all of them squatting in a circle in the dusty school playground, she heard that a pair of Java sparrows were needing a home. They belonged to the children of a family who were departing for a posting in Madras. 'Perfect!' she thought, and sought the memsahib's permission to obtain the birds as a present for Melanie.

Melanie eventually decided it was nice to have an ayah, after all.

For the first few days she was not quite sure because she had grown accustomed to looking after herself, and now Lakshmi was always close at hand, reminding her to brush her teeth and comb her hair and pull up her socks and wash her face and a thousand and one other things. But Melanie soon got used to Lakshmi's firm but gentle ways and it was very useful to have someone to carry your coat, and remember your school satchel, and make sure you had remembered to collect your sandwiches from Cook before you went to school.

And it was reassuring to know that Lakshmi would be waiting outside to take her home from school, because, before she had an ayah, she never knew who would be waiting to take her home. It might have been her mother (though not very often recently) or her father (he was usually late) or the Bearer or someone else's mother who would always look sad when she asked how Melanie's Mummy was.

Now Lakshmi was there, insisting on holding her hand to make sure she was safe: which was mostly nice, but often a bit of a nuisance because Melanie wanted to run and play hide and seek in the gardens and not walk properly like a little lady. So sometimes she would snatch her hand from Lakshmi's and dash off to hide. Her favourite place was under the rhododendrons — not her old den, because Mummy had told Lakshmi where that was, but down by the lake in the gardens.

Her mother had promised that Melanie would like Bombay. And Melanie thought she did. Well, mostly, anyway. She missed Kelly and the rabbits and the garden and the hens. In Bombay they didn't live in a house but in a big airy flat that was part of a block built on Malabar Hill where the air was clean and clear and sunlight filled the windows all through the day.

Round the big building stretched a beautiful garden full of scented shrubs and flowers of all kinds and colours. Melanie particularly liked the red, yellow and purple ones. There was a huge lawn where you could play croquet or have picnics and a lake with all sorts of water birds swimming in it. Boats were drawn up on the boat ramp but children were not allowed to play in them, which Melanie felt was most unfair until Lakshmi explained that boats were dangerous and might sink and drown little girls, especially if they couldn't swim very well, so you could only go in a boat if your Daddy was with you. Even Mummies weren't allowed in the boats on their own, Lakshmi said.

On Sundays, Lakshmi had her day off and either Mummy looked after Melanie, which was lovely because they played snap or canasta or monopoly or mahjong (which was Melanie's favourite), or Daddy would take her to play on the swings in the children's area outside his club. Melanie liked that best of all because usually Alan was there, and sometimes Derek. They were a whole year older than her, but they let her pretend she was a boy and play cowboys and indians with them or, when she insisted on a change, doctors and nurses. The one game they would not play was mummies and daddies, but that didn't matter because she played that a lot at home anyway, and she didn't really want to have boys playing with her special dolls or their tea set (which had teeny-weeny little cups and saucers and plates with pink roses on), and everyone knew that boys didn't push doll's prams or put doll children to bed or give them medicine.

Melanie was surprised at how happy she was when Lakshmi came back on that first Sunday evening in time to sit with her at the dining table while she ate her high tea. Mummy was sitting in a chair by the window, reading, although her head was at a funny angle and Melanie knew she was sleeping because her eyes were closed and she made a funny little sound in her throat like a kitten purring. Lakshmi knew she was sleeping, too, because when Melanie opened her mouth to speak, Lakshmi put her fingers to her lips and said she must whisper.

When Melanie had finished eating, she and her ayah tiptoed out onto the veranda. Lakshmi told the little girl to close her eyes tight behind her hands, but Melanie peeped through her fingers and saw something so wonderful that she gasped, and Lakshmi giggled, and then Mummy woke up too and smiled. For there on the veranda, Lakshmi — nodding, smiling and giggling all at once — was holding up a round wicker cage, over which was draped a blue cloth. She whipped the cloth from the cage with a flourish to reveal two beautiful little black Java sparrows with mother-of-pearl beaks. The birds hopped about the cage for a minute or two while Melanie watched with round eyes and open mouth, and then they began to sing, so prettily and so sweetly that Melanie knew they had come to her straight from Heaven.

Later, her mother told Melanie that Lakshmi had gone to great trouble to obtain the Java sparrows for her so it was important that she looked after them very, very carefully. But Melanie had known from the moment she had set eyes on the birds that they were a very special gift for her. Maybe Lakshmi and Melanie each recognised the other's inner loneliness, but no matter, for the gift of the songbirds strengthened the bond between them.

- 6 -

Elephants

When Lakshmi had given the Java sparrows to Melanie, the delight in the child's eyes proved she had guessed correctly: the child needed something living to love.

Melanie did love the songbirds. Part of her wanted to set them free like the ones she had bought in Karachi, but both her mother and Lakshmi said that, if she did, the Indian birds would kill them.

"Why?" asked Melanie.

"Because they're not native here, darling. They come from a country far away from India. They have been bred by humans to sing for humans so they've always been caged. Even if the other birds didn't attack them, they wouldn't know how to survive in the wild."

Sad though she was that the birds could not be freed, Melanie didn't mind too much because the birds were very pretty and sang sweetly, and she supposed she did want to keep them where she could see them and play with them. She decided she would train them to perch on her finger, like Long John Silver's parrot in the book Treasure Island, which, she remembered, always perched on his shoulder squawking "Pieces of eight, pieces of eight."

She imagined walking around with a Java sparrow on each hand and how everyone would say: 'Look how well

Melanie has trained those Java sparrows!' But she couldn't catch them even *inside* their cage, no matter how much Cerebos Salt she poured onto their tails to make them stand still. Soon, salt covered the bottom of the birdcage which had to be cleaned out, and Melanie lapsed back into quietness.

It was then that Lakshmi thought of the elephants. Bombay Zoo possessed several. They were popular attractions throughout the year, but on special occasions the elephants came into their own. There were spectacular festivals when the huge, stately but cumbersome animals, beautifully attired and magnificently decorated, led processions of musicians, jugglers, drummers and dancers through the streets of the city.

Most of Bombay's tame elephants were mature animals, but recently Lakshmi had heard tales of a birth in the Elephant House. She had also heard rumours that the elephant calf and its mother were to be housed temporarily in the animal enclosure of the Hanging Gardens, where it was quieter than in the noisy surroundings of the city. Perhaps it would be easier to train the baby elephant away from crowds and with its mother in close attendance; or perhaps the authorities knew that, although the Gardens were a huge tourist attraction in themselves, the baby elephant would prove an even greater draw to tourists and foreigners.

The Hanging Gardens of Bombay were constructed

over a reservoir that provided water to most of the bustling, busy, over-crowded city. Situated on the top of Malabar Hill, overlooking Bombay's wide bay with its lapis lazuli ocean full of ships and smaller faster craft — the harbour being as busy and crowded as the seafront — the Gardens acted as the city's lungs. Here the air was clear and pure, for the hill caught every breath of wind from the Arabian Sea and often a breeze could be found stirring the leaves in the Gardens when, down below, the city was lost in a fog of inert, stifling pollution.

Long ago the Gardens had been laid out with trees and shrubs and, between them, paths and herbaceous borders full of flowers: a well-manicured garden full of fantastic patterns and shapes. Annuals of all colours cascaded in streams and floods of colour and the hedges were clipped into enticing shapes, mostly of animals, that held Melanie entranced.

The Gardens were also very busy. An army of gardeners, labourers and builders were required to keep it trim and perfect. No twig dared grow where it was not supposed to be: out would come a pair of shears and the shrub's outline would be perfect once again. No weed dared show a shoot: it would be instantly despatched to the compost heap. No blade of grass dared creep between the red bricks of the path: it would be scraped away immediately.

Melanie's mother said there was the very same shoe in the gardens that had once belonged to 'the old woman who lived in a shoe and had so many children she didn't know what to do'. Melanie asked exactly how many children she had? It was a silly story — how could anyone live in a shoe? Mummy thought that perhaps the old woman was a fairy, or that she and her family had been magicked small by a wicked wizard. Melanie considered this, but her logical brain decided that, if the old woman lived there with so many children, it must be a *real* house shaped like a shoe, not a shoe like the ones she was wearing.

One of the first things Lakshmi had arranged for Melanie was a daily walk in the Hanging Gardens that included a visit to the children's playground, where, sure enough, a huge concrete boot was to be found. Painted white, with a flight of stairs inside and windows looking out from the toe and the top, it boasted a small pitched roof of red tiles that balanced precariously above a small look-out place at the top. It had one or two small spaces where one might fit a child's bed, thought Melanie, but not very many. After all, according to the rhyme, 'the old woman who lived in a shoe had had so many children she didn't know what to do'. She must have fitted them in somewhere because 'she whipped them all soundly and put them to bed'. Perhaps they slept on the stairs, Melanie decided, or in hammocks like the sailors on the boat. But where did the old woman cook? 'She gave them some broth without any bread' before she whipped them so she must have cooked it up somewhere.

"Perhaps she made a fire outside," suggested Lakshmi, shivering and trying to lead her charge away from this horrible place peopled with ghosts, or at the very least reminding one of times of famine and hardship.

"And heated the soup in a big cauldron?" Melanie suggested. Possibly, she thought, walking round and round the shoe every time they visited it, but she couldn't find anywhere to build a fire, no matter how hard she looked. It must all have been a very long time ago before electricity when the old woman lived there with her children and they were probably all dead now anyway because there was no sign of anyone living in the shoe nowadays.

Melanie's brow always creased in thought after she had visited the shoe. A shoe was made of leather. Or sometimes of plastic. Why was this shoe built of concrete? Why was it so big and so incommodious? She had learned that word from her father only yesterday when she had discussed the shoe's shortcomings with him. Why did it just have openings and no proper doors and windows?

"Why did the old woman whip her children?" she would ask; and Lakshmi would shudder and say: "Because they were naughty, Missy. Now come away, come away. The elephants are waiting for you."

Melanie would streak past her in a frenzy of delight, heading for the elephants' enclosure where her friend Nelly would be expecting her. Lakshmi would grumble under her breath as she hobbled along behind, but she knew that Melanie would not run too far or too fast because the elephants were only a hundred yards distant.

"Nelly, Nelly," Melanie would call and there would come a strange little sound, almost like a sigh, but

Melanie knew it was Nelly calling her because she had introduced herself properly and had been teaching Nelly to call her name, just as she had taught Matilda to say 'Bom-ba'.

Melanie was singing now in her high little voice:
"Nelly the elephant packed her trunk,
And off she tramped to the cir ... cus,
Off she went with a trumpetty-trump,
Trump ... Trump ... Trump. "

When Lakshmi rounded the corner she would see Melanie clinging to the fence singing and the little elephant rocking from side to side only a few feet from her.

It had been a long process to reach this stage. The elephant's keeper was always present in the enclosure and he had taught Melanie how to approach the animals safely. The child learned quickly, but more than that, she possessed a real affinity with the baby elephant.

The mother elephant was used to Melanie now. At first she had been wary, always ushering her baby away from the little girl, but Melanie's patience with animals was as surprising as it was real. For day after day she simply sat on a seat close by, singing her little song and smiling and talking to the elephants, making no attempt to touch them and keeping far enough away to make sure she did not spook the mother. After perhaps fifteen minutes she would call "Goodbye, Nelly!", jump down from the seat and take Lakshmi's hand. She would gently lead Lakshmi home. On occasion it almost felt to Lakshmi that she was the child and Melanie the adult.

After a couple of weeks Melanie declared that Nelly was used to her. The keeper, flashing a white smile, agreed. Following his instructions, she crept slowly towards the fence and, from then on, she would simply talk to Nelly as if she were a friend of her own age. Gradually the elephant learned to trust the child, and the mother allowed her offspring to wander close to the fence without trying to intervene, although Lakshmi, herself keeping a wary eye on the magnificent beast, noticed that the mother elephant always watched her baby.

Finally, there came the day when the keeper allowed Melanie to offer a handful of feed to the baby elephant. Melanie's delight when the small animal clasped the end of its trunk around the handful and thrust it into its mouth, caused Lakshmi to blink back sudden tears.

The memsahib had offered Lakshmi the use of a small room, rather like a big cupboard, but the Indian woman had refused the offer much as she opined to appreciate it. She had so few possessions: her bed-roll, two short blouses, two petticoats, two saris — one for everyday wear and the other for interviews and celebrations — the nose ring, bangles and toe rings that she habitually wore, and her one luxury, a tobacco tin full of *betel* leaves. A room would have been far too big and isolated, accustomed as she was to sleeping across the doorway of a child's room, but she did accept the use of a small cupboard in which she stowed away these treasures.

At night she would remove her blouse and sari, roll out her thin mattress across the door and settle down to sleep in her underclothes. Occasionally she snored. When she did, Melanie knew that she was sound asleep; but Melanie seldom heard Lakshmi's snores because she herself generally slept very deeply even though she was frequently troubled by nightmares.

The little girl would toss and turn, crying out on the edge of sleep. It was then that she would be conscious of Lakshmi's calming presence, but otherwise she had no appreciation of the lightness of her ayah's sleep and her constant care for her.

Melanie had always dreamt vividly: her nights were filled with dreams. One, in particular, was a recurring vision she would remember all her life.

In the dream she travelled down into a cave deep in the earth, feeling held and surrounded by a great love. From there she would look up to find herself in the heavens — a huge indigo void that was yet strangely comforting, filled to the brim with sparkling, many-coloured points of light and a feeling of deep, unconditional love. She could not remember when she had first experienced this dream, but the whole experience was so familiar that she knew it had been a part of her from an early age. And, despite the problems and difficulties of everyday life that beset her, young as she was, the dream confirmed an inner knowledge that her life was secure and guided. She felt that her whole consciousness was part of a greater, immense and loving whole, but she had not the words to express this truth. Later in life she would come to realise that this was a state of altered consciousness and she would wonder whether all children came into the world trailing such ribbons of glory.

Sometimes she would ask silently to dream this dream, but it would not come to order; and instead she found herself subject to nightmares in which she would find herself taken far away from where she was comfortable and at ease. Bound so she could not move, imprisoned in a box too small for her size, hot, thirsty and hungry, she would wake longing for cool water, luscious green leaves and the cool shade of trees.

Or she would find herself bound and unable to move. It was as if she had four feet and one front and one back were chained to something deep within the ground. She would strain and strain against the chains, feel them biting deep into her flesh, but still she was unable to move more than a foot or two in any direction. Longing for freedom and the coolness of trees, trying to pull herself free, making pitiful cries of helplessness. Longing and trying. Trying and crying. Until she feels herself surrender, give in to the pain and helplessness. Feels her wild tortured spirit broken.

When she woke, her voice would be hoarse from screaming and her body tangled in the bed sheet. Usually Lakshmi — but sometimes Mummy — would be holding her, smoothing her brow, offering her a sip of water and she would turn into a motherly shoulder and cry great watery tears of rage and pain and longing. But in the morning, she would wake blithe and happy as usual, singing her little songs and smiling.

Her mother asked her about the horrible dreams but

Melanie could not remember anything about them apart from the fact that she liked waking to find her or Lakshmi beside her. Her mother said it was probably as well that she didn't remember: it was probably something that she had eaten — perhaps onions didn't agree with her? Melanie could not remember eating onions. She didn't like them much: their texture was too slimy-wet, they made your eyes run, your tongue burn and your breath smell — at least, they made Daddy's breath smell because he was very partial to raw onions.

Then one morning Melanie woke up in the middle of a dream, but she did not open her eyes. She let herself be pulled back into the dream, still half-awake. She was so happy, so full of joy in her surroundings, in simply being.

She felt her heart singing in her chest as she wandered on a hillside in a wilderness of green trees and small bushes: she raised her eyes to the heavens to watch the lazy flight of a bird-of-prey, her legs swinging easily as she trampled greenness underfoot. To her ears came the sound of the rushing water she had smelled as she walked. She was thirsty but she did not walk any faster. Her mother would look after her, she knew; she could smell her mother's closeness and that made her hungry. A drink of milk would be perfect.

There was something odd about her eyes because she was looking more out to the side. In fact, she could see almost all the way round her head without moving it and a little bit of her nose, too, which was long and grey and swung when she walked. She was an elephant!

"Wake up, Missy!" Lakshmi's intruding voice seemed

very far away. Melanie frowned and buried her head in her pillow but the dream was fading fast. All that she remembered was that she had dreamed she was an elephant.

"Missy! Wake up! Time for school!"

Melanie scowled at Lakshmi and punched the offending pillow but it didn't make any difference. So she slid to the floor and stamped her way to the bathroom to clean her teeth. Lakshmi heard her singing.

"Nelly the elephant ... "

After that, dreams and daydreams came thick and fast and Melanie was able to drift in and out of them more or less at will. When she went to visit Nelly, she would sit cross-legged on the ground near the fence, close her eyes and let her mind go blank. Soon she would find her head filled with images and emotions that were as strange to her as they felt familiar.

She became dreamy and apparently listless, and yet when she was present she was happier than Lakshmi had ever known her to be. She wondered whether she should say anything to Memsahib but Lakshmi had heard from the Bearer that the doctor was visiting the memsahib every day and talking to Sahib about her being very-greatly ill, so she kept quiet.

One day, the memsahib called Lakshmi to her.

"I want to thank you, Lakshmi," she said, her voice so dreamy that Lakshmi knew she had taken a lot of medicine to deaden her pain. "You have made so much difference to Melanie. I know she's day-dreaming a lot, but she's so much happier. And her grades at school are much better, too."

Relief made Lakshmi giggle as she tendered her very-great thanks to Memsahib for not forgetting of her.

"I could never forget you, Lakshmi. And nor will Melanie, I know." She smiled: a sad, wistful smile. "But I have to speak to you seriously. I have to go into hospital for some weeks and I will need you to take special care of Melanie while I'm away. Of course, I will tell her where I am going. But she will not be allowed to visit me for several days, so I know she will be unsettled."

Lakshmi made a sound in her throat and in her dark brown eyes Elizabeth saw a depth of perception that she had rarely encountered. The older woman steepled her hands together and bowed.

"Of course, I will take very-great care of her, Memsahib."

"It has been so good that you have taken her to see the elephants every day. It seems she has a particular affinity ...." Seeing Lakshmi's puzzled expression, Elizabeth paused. "I mean, she loves the creatures. Please continue to take her to see them. I feel sure they will help her while I am away, don't you?"

"Indeed, I do, Memsahib."

Now that she had been given the memsahib's blessing, Lakshmi had no scruples about taking Melanie to see her elephant friends as often as the child wished.

It was less than two days later that the memsahib went into hospital.

In the morning Melanie had sat on her mother's bed

and listened very carefully to what her mother told her. Afterwards, Elizabeth hugged her daughter and told her that she would soon be well again and they could go on long walks and for picnics. But for the next few days she must be very brave, because the one thing that would help her to get better was to know that Melanie was happy. And she must be good for Lakshmi too.

Melanie hugged her mother back, drying the odd tear that she couldn't sniff away on the shoulder of Mummy's bed jacket. Then her mother suggested that the Java sparrows needed to be fed and Melanie went onto the balcony where she murmured her worry and doubts to the birds as she fed them.

She recounted to them what her mother had said and that she didn't like the sound of it at all. The doctors were going to cut Mummy open to see if there was anything wrong. If there wasn't they would just sew her up again and send her home quite soon afterwards, but if there was something wrong they would cut more of her away before they sewed her up and she would have to stay in hospital until it had all healed up. Mummy said that the doctors would give her something to make her sleep so she would not feel any pain when she was cut open. In fact she would be asleep.

Asleep? Melanie couldn't believe it. When she had only pricked her finger on a thorn it hurt a lot, and when she had cut her leg on a piece of jagged glass it hurt very much indeed for a very long time. How could Mummy sleep through the doctors cutting her tummy open? She did not truly believe this story. She thought it was a fib. A fib like the one her mother had told her before — about how your eyes dried up when you were an adult so adults couldn't cry. That had been a great *big* fib! She knew that because Mummy had wept so much when Granny had got ill and died.

Oh no! Surely Mummy wasn't going to die? Hadn't Mummy said that Granny had died in hospital in England? Oh no! She couldn't bear to be without her lovely, kind, pretty Mummy. Not now! Not *ever*! The dark feeling was all over her again and she could feel her heart beating so hard and fast in her chest that she couldn't breathe.

Her mother had told her she must be brave and smile because she needed to know that Melanie was happy. But how could she smile and be happy when Mummy was going to be cut open?

When Lakshmi eventually found her, hidden deep inside the rhododendron bush, Melanie had sobbed herself into acceptance. She was more than ready to come out. In fact, for some time the little girl had been hoping that Lakshmi would find her. The ayah's presence was comforting and her scent even more so. Melanie hid her face in Lakshmi's sari and concealed herself behind the ayah's bulk as the two of them slipped unseen back into the flat and into the bathroom. The ayah had already drawn Melanie a warm bath and now she gently stripped the little girl of her dirty clothes and helped her into the bath. She tenderly bathed the little girl's scratched knees and elbows, gently swabbing her swollen lips and eyes, promising to take her to see the elephants directly after school tomorrow. But first she must dry her tears and put on a pretty dress and go and give her Mummy such a big hug that it would last all the time she was in hospital.

That night Melanie dreamed again. She was a great big mother elephant who had lost her little elephant child. The huge animal's rage and grief tumbled inside her small frame, mixing with the loss and hopelessness she was already feeling. The elephant had called on the rest of the small female herd to help find her baby and the herd of huge animals lumbered through the forest up hill and down hill, across fast flowing streams, through native villages, through fields and forest, along tracks known only to elephants and roads travelled only by men. In their haste and rage everything was trampled — crops, bamboo, shrubs, small trees and men — as the grief stricken mother trumpeted her longing, her grief and her wrath.

One by one the other elephants gave up the chase but the mother lumbered on ... and on ... and on. She was about to give up, to lie down and die when she heard her infant's call within her great heart and knew she was not far from finding her. On she limped until, almost dead with thirst and hunger, she came upon the camp. Moving slowly and quietly, she heaved herself through the trees. She smelled her calf, smelled its distress and fear. A squeal, a cry of pain — and she was charging through the remainder of the trees into the clearing. The baby elephant had caught her mother's scent and cried out — louder, and louder still — until the clearing rang with anguish and the sound of trampling feet.

Bang! Bang! Bang! Gunshots filled the air as small dark men ran wildly away; some shinned up trees, others took to their heels. Bang! Bang! Bang! The white man stood his ground, his gun firing constantly as the grief-deranged mother elephant charged towards him to her certain death. Her heart was bursting now. She felt the blood surge from her chest, slowing her as if her legs were caught in a swamp. She slowed. And slowed more. But her advance seemed inexorable, and the white man finally fled before her. The elephant calf smelled her mother's blood, and her sixth sense warned her of what was to come. Her squeal changed in tone, became a keening of grief like the wind screaming from the hilltops. The adult elephant's body shook in a huge dying sigh, and the animal keeled over like a great ship upon a sea of grass.

A gush of air bore the animal's spirit from her body. The earth quaked with the shock: after-tremors rocked the trees, rustling their leaves. Silence: bending trees slowly straightening. In the aftermath of death there was a great stillness. Even the calf was still now, frozen in shock as well as bound in ropes, silent in its cage. The silence stretched: and stretched further. Until slowly, slowly, men crept out from behind trees and undergrowth. Others descended from the treetops. The white man, who had fallen full length upon the ground, slowly rose and gathered up his gun.

Silent in her prison, the elephant calf grieved for her mother, her freedom, her kind. Never again, she intuited, would she be free to roam the green and sacred land.

Never again would she watch a lazy bird-of-prey circle between the green jungle hills; never again would she play with her kind in the crystal waters of the creeks — squirting water, bathing, drinking, playing. Ever after, she would be at the mercy of man, this puny creature who would beat and poke the spirit from her, until she did his bidding always.

When Melanie woke in the morning the dream was still upon her. A great weight crushed against her heart and she felt the agony of mother and child in every pore of her being, but she did not weep for the grief was too deep, too real for tears. And today was the day her mother was going away. It was her grief too.

Lakshmi understood and quietly prepared the child for school. Melanie submitted to the hair brushing and face washing and the doing-up-of-buttons, but remained pallid and lacklustre despite these ministrations. Her goodbye to her mother was drained and awkward. In vain did Lakshmi chatter, then admonish and finally cajole. Melanie went sullenly to school, veiled in a cloak of dark despair and Lakshmi's heart felt close to breaking.

Ganesha

Melanie was unusually silent when her ayah collected her from school that afternoon. Making no pretence of interacting with her peers, she simply took Lakshmi's hand and led her towards the elephants' enclosure in the Hanging Gardens.

For once, it was deserted of visitors. Only the young mahout was there, on the other side of the fence. Seeing her, he smiled and said something to the elephant. Immediately the huge animal's trunk caught him round the waist and deposited him on her back, just behind her head. The man stood up and waved at Melanie before issuing another command at which the elephant raised her front leg. The mahout slid down from behind her ear and, using the elephant's knee as a step, jumped down to the ground and bowed to his audience of one little girl.

Melanie tried to smile. But she did not really feel like it, so, leaning back against the fence, she put her left thumb in her mouth and twisted a finger of the other hand in her hair — and there she stayed, sucking and twisting. Huge tears glistened in her eyes before running messily down her cheeks.

Full of concern for the small child, Lakshmi squatted nearby. The mahout, seeing her anxiety, left the elephant's enclosure and came to squat quietly beside her. The Indian woman made no acknowledgement of his presence and the mahout, wise beyond his years, remained still and quiet beside her.

Eventually, Lakshmi glanced at him and he noticed that, although her eyes were brimming with dismay, wisdom, seasoned with a hint of laughter, lurked in their depths. She held the end of her sari across her lower face, so he could see nothing but those eyes. Realising this, he also realised how unconventional it was for them to be squatting side-by-side when there was no familial tie between them.

"The elephants will come," he said in Hindi. "That is what she is waiting for."

"I know,"Lakshmi whispered back in the same language. "But will it be enough?"

One large tear rolled down her wrinkled cheek and dropped onto her sari. She wiped the back of her hand across her eyes, and sniffed into the sari covering her lower face.

"It will be enough," her companion said, turning to watch the silent child. "She is an elephant girl. They speak to her."

"But she's a foreigner," Lakshmi rejoined. "What can she know of elephants? Surely you have been with elephants all your life? Is it not true that those who deal with elephants come from elephant country? Was not your father a mahout and your father's father before him?"

"Indeed, it is true! I come from a long, long line of mahouts who have worked with elephants for generation after generation. I, myself, did not wish to be an elephant boy. No, indeed, I can tell you! That was not in my mind ever at all. But then my father is giving me my very-own elephant to care for and she is caring for me. After that, I am unable to run away. I am shackled: my elephant is holding me. You are seeing? She was deciding that I was the very-best boy for her: and I am bowing to the hand of Fate." He smiled, but Lakshmi said nothing. "You are seeing that my elephant was choosing me? That is the way with elephants. We can do many things and they can do many things, but in the end it is the elephant does the choosing."

"And you are thinking they will choose my Missy?"

The mahout waggled his head in that most Indian of gestures. "I am not thinking: I am knowing. And the choosing, it is done! Look there."

Melanie was standing on the fence now, regarding the baby elephant whose eyes were on a level with hers. Something — empathy, intuition, an inner knowing perhaps — flashed from one to the other and back again. Still keeping the eye-contact with the elephant calf, Melanie pushed her hand through the bars of the fence, offering a fistful of hay. The elephant sniffed the offering delicately with her trunk before taking it gently from the little girl and, throwing its head back, stuffing the food into its mouth. The trunk found its way back though the bars like a large grey snake, sniffing Melanie from top to bottom and back again from bottom to top, its pink-lined proboscis skimming sweetly over her clothes until it came to her hand. Next moment the trunk had firmly grasped Melanie's hand. The little girl gasped and giggled in sheer delight.

The older female elephants in the enclosure had been watching this calmly, in much the same way as Lakshmi herself. Now they returned to their food, but not before Lakshmi had seen what she guessed was a look of approval. The thought brought her back to the present and to her responsibilities. She rose to her feet and was about to intervene when she heard the mahout say:

"Elephants are wise and noble creatures, you are seeing? They are as conscious as a guru is. They are knowing what a person is thinking: and they are knowing when a person is not doing what he is thinking. A person can trust an elephant: but an elephant cannot trust a person."

"I understand," Lakshmi responded. "But does Missy?"

"Your Missy is not needing understanding. She is needing loving: and the elephants are loving her."

Lakshmi smiled. "Ganesha," she whispered.

"Now indeed you are talking!" responded the mahout, flashing his extraordinarily white teeth in a grin. "It is time to tell her of Ganesha."

Melanie was in seventh heaven. All around her was the smell of elephants and the feel of elephants. Nelly's trunk was alternately tickling and squeezing her hand, and the mother elephant's trunk was sniff-searching her face, before coming to rest around her shoulders. But most of all she could hear the thinking of elephants: and the thoughts of elephants were happy and funny and sad and poignant and kind and teasing and just a little bit annoying because they were thinking quite a lot about food.

She laughed happily, blowing softly in the baby elephant's face. The baby elephant snorted, raised its trunk and blew right back at Melanie. The child found herself showered in elephant spit and thought it was the funniest thing that had ever happened to her.

Lakshmi shrugged at the thought of washing the girl's dress. Seeing her happy, if only for a short while, was worth the labour. She giggled: and Melanie glanced at her, waved and giggled, too.

A short time later, a group of tourists straggled in, gossiping and gesticulating. The elephants moved away from Melanie, no doubt feeling happier away from the raucous humans. The little girl ran back to her ayah and threw her arms round Lakshmi's waist. She prattled gaily about elephants all the way home, all through her high tea and all the time she was in the bath.

The only time her smile slipped was when her father came in to read her the story that her mother usually read. But that was alright because him reading to her was a special treat and she could always prevail on him to read her another story and another … and tickle her until she was breathless. Then he would tuck the sheet round her much tighter than her mother did, kiss her brow and say goodnight in Burmese. Yes, it was very special to have her father read her a bedtime story but he forgot to say prayers with her.

She wriggled out of bed, knelt beside it with her hands together and said them straight away before she forgot. She said a special prayer for Mummy and another for the elephants, snuggled back beneath the sheet and was asleep almost as soon as her head touched the pillow.

Lakshmi told Melanie the legend of Ganesha and in turn she regaled her mother with the legend the second time she was taken to visit her in hospital.

Melanie was not really supposed to be there because children weren't normally allowed, but she had begged and begged and in the end her father had made the arrangements — but only for a short visit. The first five minutes passed in a flash as Melanie gabbled on about the elephants and all the unshed tears she felt coming from them.

She said she thought the tears must dry up somewhere between the elephant's eyes and the end of their trunks, because, although she had noticed that their eyes were often red, she had never seen real tears running down their faces. She thought that maybe their tears did dry up when they were older, and maybe it was only when your Mummy died that you cried real tears as an adult. And anyway if they came down the elephants' noses like they came down hers, making her sniff a lot, the elephant's tears would have an awful lot of nose to fill up.

When her mother asked why she thought the elephants were crying, her daughter told her all the details of her dream and added that the mahout of the elephants in the Hanging Gardens had told Lakshmi she was an 'Elephant's Child' which meant that she could communicate with them without talking. She wasn't quite sure what 'communicate' meant, but she always knew what the elephants were thinking and it was often quite surprising, although they did think about food an awful lot and that was really boring. They understood about being sad and her wanting to see Mummy well and happy again.

The little girl hadn't stopped talking from the moment she'd run to her mother's bedside. She was sitting on the edge of the hospital bed now, swinging her legs, and kissing her mother's hand by way of punctuation when she paused for breath. Her father had told her that sitting on the bed was forbidden to visitors in the ordinary course of events, but that he would distract the nurse by talking to her about her feet.

All too soon it was time to go — and she still hadn't told Mummy about Ganesha.

"Never mind," said Lakshmi. "Why don't you draw her a picture instead?"

So Melanie drew a special picture of a beautiful goddess with four arms and a little boy with an elephant's head, sitting in a garden surrounded by flowers. She coloured all the flowers very carefully, but she was tired when she came to colour the elephant's head and it was boring grey anyway so she was a little careless about crayoning over the pencilled edges. Lakshmi said it didn't matter, because it was a beautiful picture, drawn and coloured with love; Mummy would love it and would quite understand if it wasn't absolutely perfectly coloured in. But Melanie was annoyed with herself and set about redrawing and colouring the picture until it was perfect, or as near as could be. After all, she was drawing a goddess and a god so it had to be the very best she could do!

Sure enough, her mother was delighted with the drawing and asked her daughter to explain what it was about.

"Once there was a beautiful goddess named Parvati. She had four arms because she liked giving so much that she needed four hands to give away all the things that people needed. She always knows what you need, you see. Lakshmi says that she gives things you can't see, like health and happiness, and that she is always near us but we can't see her." Elizabeth nodded seriously as her daughter hurried on.

"Parvati was married to the chief of the gods, Shiva, and they were very happy because they loved each other very much. Parvati was often sad when Shiva wasn't there — just like you're sad when Daddy isn't there. But Parvati wasn't sad because she was ill or hurting like you, Mummy ..." Here Melanie gave her mother's hand a quick butterfly kiss with her eyelashes, before continuing. "She was sad because she wanted a son and she hadn't got one. She waited for a while to see if she would have one, but no baby came. So when Shiva went away for a week or two Parvati made a son out of clay — the way a potter does, Lakshmi says, because Parvati was a great artist — and breathed life into him."

"Ah!" said Mummy, wisely refraining from

interrupting her daughter's breathless flow of words.

"Parvati called her son Ganesha (which means Lord of many things) and because he was a goddess's son he grew very fast — less than a *day* — into a man. Lakshmi says he was a very, very handsome man. And Parvati loved him as much as she loved Shiva — which Lakshmi says was *very* dangerous because Gods can be *particularly* jealous. Parvati was very happy and could not wait for Shiva to come home and see his son. When she heard that Shiva was coming she wanted to look beautiful for him so she decided to have a bath before she got dressed in her most beautiful sari — which I think must have been red and gold because those colours go so beautifully together, don't they? She must have had lots and lots of gold jewellery, don't you think, Mummy?"

Melanie paused to hiccough, having run out of breath. She didn't pause long enough for her mother to answer, but she noticed that Mummy had a lovely wide smile on her face.

"Anyway, Parvati asked Ganesha to stand guard, because she was very beautiful and lots of men wanted to peep at her when she was naked. But Shiva came home while Parvati was still in the bath and Ganesha refused to allow him to go in. Shiva was *extremely* angry and cut off Ganesha's head with his sword. When Parvati found her son dead without a head, she wept and wept — and *I* think she would have been very cross with Shiva, too, don't you?"

"I think that's very probable," her mother agreed.

"Shiva said he was sorry and he would find another

head for Ganesha and bring him back to life — which he *could* do because he was the god of Life, although I think it would have been much easier to stick Ganesha's own head back on his body! But no! Shiva went off to find another head. And the first one he came across belonged to an elephant! The elephant was travelling north, which was a very good omen because north is the direction of wisdom, Lakshmi says. So Shiva cut off the elephant's head — which I think must have killed the elephant, but Lakshmi says it didn't because the elephant's life and wisdom stayed in the head — and put it on Ganesha's body."

"And this is Ganesha?" her mother asked, pointing to the figure in Melanie's drawing.

"Of course!" the child agreed, a trifle scornfully. "He's got four arms like his mother and an elephant's head!"

"And do you know anything else about Ganesh?"

"Gan*esha*, Mummy! Yes, he has an elephant's head to show he is wise and clever: his trunk is so strong he can pick up a tree and so fine he can use it to thread a needle — although he has four hands already, so I don't know why he would want to use his trunk for *that* — but what he does best is to remove obstacles. So if anything is wrong you can ask him to help you to move it out of your way. But I'm not quite sure what an obstacle is, Mummy?"

"It's something that stops you from doing something else, like ..."

"Like getting well? That's what Lakshmi said."

"Yes, darling, like getting well or being happy,

perhaps."

"I do so want you to get well, Mummy, so we can all be happy again."

"I know, darling. I'm trying very hard."

"So you can ask him to remove your obstacle, Mummy. Lakshmi said there's a special sort of prayer that you say over and over again. It's called a mantra and there's a special one you say to ask Ganesha ..."

But at that moment her father came in and told her to say goodbye quickly because Lakshmi was waiting to take her home, and it was only later that Melanie realised she hadn't told Mummy the magic words: there was nothing else for it, she would have to say them herself. She would ask Lakshmi if that would be all right.

Lakshmi agreed that if her mother couldn't say the words herself, it was all right because you could do it for someone else. Melanie understood this: a mantra must be like a prayer — not completely like a prayer of course, because prayers were said in old-fashioned English words and you always had to say 'four-Jesus-cries-ache' at the end. Melanie had often wondered why the prayer ended this way. Now she considered that perhaps there were four Jesuses, like the four arms that Parvati and Ganesha possessed. And maybe He 'cried ' because his arms were aching on the cross.

She shuddered: she didn't like to think of Jesus on the cross. She liked Christmas when Jesus was born as a gift to the world, but she didn't understand about Good Friday and Easter at all, even though it was nice to make an Easter garden and eat lots of chocolate. When her mother was better she would ask her to explain again, but in the meantime, as well as praying to Jesus like Mummy wanted her to, she would try asking Ganesha to make her mother better.

It was very easy, Lakshmi said. You just had to keep repeating the words 'Om Gum Ganapatayei Namaha' over and over and over again. And you didn't even have to say the words out loud, you could say them in your head when you were doing something boring like arithmetic or French or waiting for Daddy. Lakshmi said the mantra was more effective if you didn't say it out loud; so she and Lakshmi would chant the words quietly together under their breath on the walk to and from school and when they were walking together in the Hanging Gardens. Melanie knew the elephants really, really liked the words because they told her so. In fact, her communication with the elephants became so clear and real that often she forgot they were animals: she thought of them as her best friends.

'Om Gum Ganapatayei Namaha' The words beat a refrain in Melanie's head. And Mummy was getting better! She would be home soon.

'Om Gum Ganapatayei Namaha' Not only that, but she forgot to be bored in arithmetic and French and her marks were improving fast.

'Om Gum Ganapatayei Namaha'. Waiting for Daddy wasn't so boring, she thought, even when the boys weren't around to play with, because there were so many other things to think about.

She thought most about elephants and what the mahout had told her of the things they were trained to do. They were clever animals, patient and wise — except sometimes when they felt playful when they could be mischievous; and occasionally when they were in musth because then they were very, very dangerous so no-one could go near them, not even their mahouts. Melanie wasn't sure what 'musth' was, but it sounded exciting. Anyway, it didn't happen very often and only to middle-aged male elephants — and Melanie didn't know any of those.

Soon after Melanie started chanting Ganesha's mantra, her mother came home. She was delicate and mostly stayed in bed or lay on the sofa, but there was colour in her cheeks and her eyes had lost their dullness so the child was sure she would soon be completely well again. Melanie asked the elephants how soon that would be: they answered that it would be sooner rather than later provided she kept on chanting 'Om Gum Ganapatayei Namaha'. Despite the fact that her friends and other children laughed at her, or told her chanting was unchristian and they would tell their mothers, Melanie chanted nearly all the time now, in her head or under her breath, but only occasionally out loud — when she knew she was out of earshot of all but Indian people and the elephants.

Lakshmi was worried. She spoke to the mahout.

"I do not think I should have taught her that mantra. She is being teased monumentally. I am only her ayah."

She was wringing her hands, her usually open countenance creased in an anxious frown. "What do I know of Christian teaching? I worry what Memsahib will do if she is finding out."

"I am most surprised that you will be thinking that," he responded. "Is Ganesha not the most powerful of gods? Will he not be removing all obstacles even as we speak?"

In truth, Elizabeth Russell, although brought up in the Christian faith and determined that her daughter should be ruled by its maxim of 'Love thy neighbour', was not enamoured of the more fundamental ideals of Protestant zeal. She could not but notice the small miracle that had been wrought in her precious daughter. The child was far more confident, far less anxious and seemed to have acquired what she could only describe as 'an inner peace.' At first, she had thought it was the elephants alone who had wrought this change, but gradually she understood that there was more to it than she had imagined.

One evening, as Elizabeth was reading *Barbar the Elephant* to her daughter, Melanie interrupted the story — something that she seldom did because she loved to listen intently — to tell her that elephants didn't actually behave like Barbar in real life. She said this almost as if she did not wish to shatter Elizabeth's illusions, forcing her mother to feign amazement while concealing her smile behind her hand.

Melanie went on to explain very carefully about Ganesha's mantra, telling her how it helped to remove obstacles, just like elephants moved trees out of the way with their trunks. She also told her that the elephants liked the mantra and that they wanted to meet Mummy when she was better enough to go for a walk in the Hanging Gardens.

When Melanie was tucked up in her bed and already half asleep, Elizabeth asked Lakshmi to come and see her. At this unusual summons, Lakshmi felt her bulk quivering with anxiety, but to her surprise the memsahib thanked her very sincerely for giving Melanie such a helpful tool. She also asked Lakshmi to teach her the chant so that she and Melanie could chant it together.

A week later, she took Melanie to see the elephants, or rather, Melanie led her there, as usual chattering all the way to the elephants' enclosure. Lakshmi followed behind, despite the memsahib's invitation to take Melanie's other hand: she knew her place.

Over the next few weeks, it gradually became the custom for Elizabeth to take Melanie for a walk in the Hanging Gardens, with Lakshmi following along behind. Elizabeth would point out the wonderful blue of the Arabian sea with the foaming waves forming a thin sparkling white necklace round the bay. Or, when the sea was choppy, the white horses' manes would show as the waves cantered in towards the shore. There were so many wonderful things to see, and her mother made them so much more exciting than Lakshmi, who was always kind and often giggly but simply not Mummy.

Melanie had always loved the sight of the bushes and hedges that were carefully clipped into the shape of animals, but she was not always sure which animals they represented. Her mother always knew: and she always had a story to tell about the rhinoceros (why he was always bad-tempered), or the leopard (how he got his spots), or the camel (why he had a hump). She even had a story about how the elephant got her trunk, but Melanie only listened to that one with half an ear because she knew it was a fairy tale.

Now that Nelly was bigger, the mahout would walk the elephants through the Gardens. Melanie loved to see the small man walking between the huge animals, for even Nelly was taller than the Mahout: she was growing fast now, noticeably bigger as day succeeded day. The mahout would always stop, holding onto their ropes so that Melanie and Mummy could have a chat with the elephants, or give them a pat. Sometimes the mahout was carrying a treat for the elephants which he would pass secretly to Melanie so that she could pretend she had brought it for her friends. The conversation would not last long, probably five minutes at most, but both humans and elephants would benefit from the encounter, all of them feeling a sense of kinship.

From time to time they would visit the elephants' enclosure. While mother and daughter spoke to the elephants and each other, if the mahout was not busy he would come and have a word with Lakshmi.

"See," he would say, "I am always telling you that the elephants are knowing what to do best. And Ganesha is always removing of obstacles."

And Lakshmi would sigh and say. "It is very true.

And soon they will be taking the ship and returning to England." Each day, the prospect depressed her a little more, for she had not only grown too fond of Melanie, she had never before encountered a memsahib who asked to be taught a mantra.

Slowly, the elephants seemed to let go of their dreaming recollections of the forest: gradually they settled back into the plodding monotony of everyday life: by degrees Melanie's reliance on the great animals for friendship and understanding changed as she spent more time in her mother's company. For Mummy was well now, healthier than she had been for a long time.

All too soon, the monsoon was upon them, with wide tumbling dark clouds and incessant rain. The rain was warm and the atmosphere so humid that clothes stuck to the body almost before they were worn. Lakshmi carried an umbrella when she collected Melanie from school, but it was useless, because the rain came down so hard that it bounced up from the pavement. Walking in the Hanging Gardens was forbidden and Melanie grew restless and grumpy. She missed the elephants, and the special time walking with her mother.

Everywhere was pervaded by damp and humidity causing discomfort for everyone and a shortness of temper. As expected, with the monsoon had come malaria and also another illness, a fever accompanied by a red rash.

Melanie's father was shivering with fever. 'A touch of malaria' he called it. Although he went to work each day, he would go straight to bed when he came home, often without eating dinner. He was always either sweating with internal heat or shivering with a bone-deep cold that turned his nose blue. Eventually he allowed Elizabeth to call the doctor, who prescribed a stronger dose of quinine. After that he gradually turned the corner and began to recover. Elizabeth herself had had the fever-with-a rash, but she too was recovering slowly, promising Melanie that she would be back to normal very soon.

As is the way with children, one minute Melanie was healthy and the next she was ill — hot, sweaty and feverish.

The rash came out fast, itchy blotches that covered her from head to toe. Her head was on fire, she thought, but did fires itch like that? Her eyes were all swimmy and she couldn't quite see anything she was looking at. The floor tilted and rocked in a surprising and sick-making way. Lakshmi whisked her into bed and stayed with her, bathing her forehead and arms with cool water, gently massaging her scalp, crooning to her in a strange flat voice that seemed to go on forever, soothing her to restless sleep.

Melanie was running through a green forest full of tall trees and thick ground creepers that snatched at her ankles as she ran. Something very hot that crackled and sang was pursuing her. She was feverish and sweaty: insects were biting her all over. Great big mosquitos. And now snakes too. Little fast black ones with hissing open mouths and thin darting tongues. She stumbled on, feeling herself panting for air, her throat sore as if she had eaten something far too hot. Her breath failed. She tried to breathe in but there was no air. She couldn't breathe!

As she sobbed and arched her back trying to catch a breath, the creepers reached out, growing so fast — as fast and big as Jack's beanstalk of the fairy tale. There was no room for her in the forest or in the world. They whipped round her body, binding her arms to her sides until she couldn't move. And now she saw that the creepers weren't plants. A massive snake was twined around her, crushing, crushing ....

She thrashed and turned and talked and cried and screamed but no-one came, no-one listened.

And then she was suddenly released. A shuddering gulp of air reached her lungs. She gasped as a great grey trunk pulled the last of the snake's coils from her, and lifted her up. The elephant's smell was reassuringly strong in her nostrils. She was still hot, still slippery; but she wasn't afraid anymore. The elephant ran with her, ran away from the pursuing fire. She felt cooler and cooler. Then the elephant was in her bedroom, laying her down gently on her bed. Feeling warm, safe and protected she slipped into fitful sleep.

She was shivering. Shivering so hard that she heard her teeth chattering in her head and felt the quivers that ran throughout her body. There was no end to them, no sooner had one started than another came and then another and she was shaking and her mouth wouldn't open and she was frightened. So frightened. She wanted the elephant to come back: but Lakshmi was there, smelling of Lakshmi and her hands were soft and soothing and cool. And Melanie drifted back to sleep.

There followed several days when the child drifted in and out of fever and hallucinations. The rash stayed hot and sore and extended down her throat and into her nose: it caused corpuscles within her hair that bled if her hair was brushed or combed and it was almost impossible to prevent the little girl from scratching.

Her mother and Lakshmi nursed her day and night, taking it in turns to sleep, although the ayah tried not to wake the memsahib since she herself was far from well. Lakshmi, too, developed a fever but she was used to such things and at her age they caused her comparatively little discomfort: she was grateful that she was not affected by the rash. Nonetheless, waiting for Melanie's fever to abate was physically and emotionally exhausting. A week passed. And another. The doctor called daily but none of his medicines availed the little girl who grew thinner and weaker by the hour.

One night, Lakshmi was sitting by Melanie's bed, drifting off into a reverie with Ganesha's mantra on her lips when she noticed a change in the child's condition. She jerked fully awake.

Melanie was dreaming — a vividly coloured dream from which there was no escape. Nightmarish scenario followed nightmarish scenario without pause.

She was an elephant crashing through the forest: men were pursuing her on great noisy beasts that belched fire and smoke: guns spoke and her whole flesh was punctured by wounds; itchy welts raised on her grey skin and a gash from knee to shoulder leaked blood as crimson and gushing as a fiery sunset over the sea.

She was walking with her mother in the Hanging Gardens, looking out to sea and watching the sun slip into a caldron of fire. The earth was shaking, collapsing beneath them: she tried to warn Mummy but no sound came. She was slipping, sliding down the mountain: she could feel it spewing fire; flames engulfed her. She had never felt so hot, her skin was burning, peeling away from her hands. She regarded them with horror. Mummy. Where was Mummy? She saw her away in the distance reaching towards her. Mummy's lips were rounded in a scream that reached right up to her terrified eyes. Melanie could hear no sound against the thumping roaring drumming beat in her head. She tried to put her hands over her ears to drown out the sound but she was pinned down, her arms would not move, could not move. The earth was swallowing her.

Now she was being smothered. A great weight crushed her down, down into the earth: the hot, hot earth was consuming her. She was dying. She bucked and arched her back; she tried to scream but there was something in her mouth stifling her voice.

Then from a great distant she heard a thundering like many, many feet running, a high wailing and the smell of elephants, earth, the forest. Water soaked her, she was wet, running with water: sweet, cooling water that ran from her body and soaked through the place beneath her. She felt the soft, searching touch of an elephant's trunk stroking her face, smelled elephant breath, and knew that she was safe. The elephants had found her, brought her back from the brink of death. A loud high-pitched keening sound close to her ear made her wince, but it was only the elephant trumpeting her joy. An elephant's trunk reached down, clasped her round her middle and raised her high in the air, carrying her gently to settle her down behind her elephant ears. But the ears weren't there, only space. Nothing.

Then there was water: cold, ice cold water all around her. She gasped and her breath stopped, caught in her body. She bucked. Breath expelled from her lungs with force. She coughed, and coughing and choking, her arms wheeled and her legs kicked.

She must swim, but something, *someone*, was holding her still. Terrified now, she stopped struggling, felt her body go limp. Found herself lifted up, felt the roughness of a towel against her face, the comfort of a lap, the familiar smells of her mother and her ayah. She turned her head into her mother's shoulder and allowed Lakshmi to remove her soaking nightdress.

Too cool now, she pressed herself into her mother's arms and allowed the ayah to towel her drenched, slippery body. A dry nightdress was passed over her head, a glass of cool water pressed to her lips … she was thirsty, so very thirsty. She tried to drink the whole glassful, but her mother restrained her, whispering "little sips, little sips."

Someone was brushing her hair. It felt soothing, calming. She knew where she was. In the bathroom, in Mummy's lap. Her mother was kissing her forehead, smoothing her hair back from her brow, whispering endearments into her ear — and behind her Lakshmi was piling sheets and blankets.

"You had a fever, darling," Mummy was saying. "You were very hot. But you're fine now. Thank Lakshmi for making you better. Now she has made you a lovely fresh bed and I will come and sleep with you to make sure you don't get too hot again."

It was years later before Melanie realised that she had nearly died that night. That convulsions had shaken her little body and she had almost stopped breathing for ever. It was Lakshmi's prompt action in heaping bed clothes on her to break the fever followed by a sudden immersion into a cold bath that had shocked her back into the land of the living.

Lakshmi had saved her life.

And the elephants had helped too: Melanie knew *that* for sure.

- 8 -

Farewell

Melanie recovered quickly as is so often the way with children. Resilient, much of the weight she had lost was soon restored and she was pleased to see that she was taller by at least an inch.

Slowly the monsoon passed away, and with it another month of the time the family had in Bombay. Soon the preparations began for their journey home to England by sea. All their possessions had to be carefully packed and labelled ready for collection. Crates and trunks would be stowed away in the ship's hold for the duration of their voyage: only small suitcases containing clothes and essential possessions were allowed in the confined space of the cabins.

The packing took weeks rather than days but eventually all was ready. Crates were piled high in each of the main rooms. A few clothes and toys remained in Melanie's cupboard and the servants moved silently around the flat, looking dismal. Mummy had been much occupied with all the labelling and packing so it had been Lakshmi who took Melanie to the Hanging Gardens. It was she who told her all about the festival of Ganesh Chaturthi which, Lakshmi said, was celebrated with great devotion all over India and in Bombay in particular.

Melanie listened, fascinated. Lakshmi had scarcely finished her account when her charge skipped along the path to tell Nelly and Nelly's mother all about it. Best of all, Lakshmi had said that the festival was about to begin in some of the temples and in many homes. It would reach its climax the day before the family were due to sail.

The elephants knew about it too, of course. They told Melanie that it was a special time of year in which they were honoured because of their connection to Ganesha. Nelly's mother had led the procession the year before Nelly was born, but she had not been allowed to take part the previous year because there were problems with her pregnancy. But this year, she would take the lead again and Nelly was excited to think that she was already being trained for the procession. She was to walk behind, holding on to her mother's tail with her trunk and she was not to let it go, whatever happened.

Both elephants would be beautifully attired and decorated with many coloured paints, beads and jewels and would carry some of the great idols of Ganesha — the elephants called them 'murtis' — in the procession. Nelly said that the murtis were huge, even bigger than she was and she had grown fast and was very big now, wasn't she? Melanie had to agree and added that *she* had grown too. Nelly thought that was a very funny thing to say because Melanie was so little, even for a human!

Melanie chattered non-stop all the way home and no sooner had they reached the gate than she deserted Lakshmi.

"Mummy, Mummy! Where are you? I have something very exciting to tell you!"

She burst into the sitting room where Elizabeth was sitting on the floor writing labels for the last items she was placing into the final crate.

"Lakshmi has told me something very exciting! Do you know it's Ganesh Chathurti already? Nelly is very excited because she's going to be in the procession when they take the murtis down to the water and she's going to hold her mother's tail all the time and not let it go — but she's big enough to remember that now so she will be alright, won't she?"

"I'm sure she will darling! Isn't that exciting?"

"Yes, and do you know that nearly all families in Bombay — well, all Hindu families — have their own little models of Ganesha in their own homes. Sometimes they make them themselves out of clay just like Parvati did when she made Ganesha all those years ago! But they have really enormous ones in the temple! And did you know they worship the murti of Ganesha? They give him food and light candles and incense and put flowers round his neck and say prayers to him. In the temples they do that every day for eleven whole days and people take offerings and say prayers and ask for Ganesha's help. Because as well as removing obstacles — like when he made you better and saved me from the rashy fever — he is very popular because he gives good fortune to everyone and even makes the weather better sometimes so people don't drown in floods in the monsoon. And ..."

Elizabeth stood up and then swooped down to ruffle her daughter's hair and kiss her brow.

"Yes, darling. It's a wonderful ceremony and we shall

go and watch the procession from the Hanging Gardens. Daddy tells me that's the best place because we will have a wonderful view of the bay from there."

Melanie clapped her hands in delight and interrupted merrily:

"Oh, that will be abso-blute-ly marb-ell-ous!" she said, mispronouncing the words in her excitement. "Because Lakshmi says that the great procession goes all round the streets to the bay and then everybody is singing and dancing and wearing bright colours of rejoicing! Then — with their big Ganeshas and their little Ganeshas — they go dancing down right into the sea and let the Ganeshas float away, back to his mother who is waiting for him with all four arms outstretched — I *think* that's what Lakshmi said — and sometimes they have candles and flowers and even *gold.* Especially gold rings because Bombay marries the sea that day, too. Do you know why Mummy?"

"What did Lakshmi say?"

"Because the sea is so important to Bombay and to all of India! But particularly to Bombay because the ships bring trade — which I think means money — as well as fish to eat. So they honour the sea as well by giving Ganesha to the ocean. Oh Mummy, I can't wait to see the procession!" And she danced up and down in delight, her sadness at leaving Bombay and Nelly, and particularly Lakshmi, almost forgotten.

On the day of the ceremony Elizabeth took Melanie up to the Hanging Gardens where they found a bench early and picnicked, surrounded by people in holiday mood bent on watching the colourful procession from the same vantage point. Everyone was happy and magnanimous, dancing and singing and drumming, sharing their food and drink generously. Joss sticks were lighted; women swirled in saris of the brightest hues, pink, red, yellow, purple, blue; hennaed patterns graced their hands and the soles of their feet were reddened too; bells jangled from all directions, the many bracelets and bangles jingling too; and from the swirling cloths the smell of jasmine, patchouli, neem, lotus, frankincense and sandalwood smothered the evening air.

The final act of giving Ganesha back to the sea was made on the outgoing afternoon tide so that the sea would take the offerings to her heart and not throw them back upon the beach. As luck would have it, the tide turned that day a little before dusk fell: the evening was balmy with a gentle breeze.

The procession started shortly after 3 o'clock, winding its way through the streets and bringing all traffic to a stop. Crowds of people attended each massive towering image from the temples: the temple Ganeshas were so huge that some even dwarfed the elephants and had to be conveyed to the sea on the backs of lorries. Melanie stood on the bench, craning her neck: she was certain she could pick out Nelly and her mother from the other elephants. Elizabeth thought that unlikely, but Melanie insisted that they were the ones who were leading the parade. All the elephants were certainly gorgeously equipped and painted in wonderful designs and colours.

"Look!" Melanie yelled suddenly. "There's Nelly! I was right! See, she's holding on to her mother's tail. Right at the front! She's playing follow-my-leader!" And she jumped up and down with excitement shouting: "Nel-ly, Nel-ly!" and Elizabeth let her shout, enjoying the child's exuberance.

Slowly the procession wound its way along the bay road. Nelly's mother carried on to the end of the road, but behind her the murtis, loaded on huge trolleys, gradually changed direction and headed down to the beach. Pulled along by willing numbers of shouting, happy volunteers, the murtis entered the water in different ways. One was stuck for a while and had to be hauled off its trolley and manhandled into the waves; others made the dash a little too fast, almost drowning some of the celebrants: but many Ganeshas were set adrift with reverence and prayers.

When the larger murtis were immersed and the procession had wound away, families brought their smaller models of Ganesha to the sea's edge and set them afloat. Soon the sky above the beautiful bay was aflame with sunset, turning the sea itself to molten flame. Amongst the gentle waves could be seen pinpoints of light, the flames of devotional candles. Even to the Hanging Gardens, high above, the fragrance of incense wafted, combined with diesel fumes and the scent of humanity.

Slowly, silence fell on the celebrants and the act of celebration became one of quiet contemplation and worship, the culmination of many days of special rites.

The sky's flames were doused in an ocean of indigo: and, as velvet violet darkness fell, a necklace of diamond-like, tiny points of flickering fire embraced the neck of the bay, while the deep silence enfolded them, one and all. One by one, candle flames died as murtis dropped to the seabed: only a precious few floated onwards on the indigo tide, slowly drifting beyond the veil of Night.

Quietly, people packed up and left. The celebrations, which had lasted two, three, five, seven or even eleven days — depending on a family's tradition — were over, although the sights and sounds would seem to hang in the air for the remainder of the year.

Those sights, the sounds, the whole amazing celebration would never be forgotten by Melanie or by Elizabeth. It was a magical and memorable end to their sojourn in India.

Although the family were leaving the following day, it wasn't quite the end. Elizabeth and Harold Russell had decided that the usual ritual of the formal goodbye to servants would only serve to make their departure more difficult, especially for Melanie. Instead, they had spoken separately to each of those who had served them, given them their 'box' — a special tip — in addition to their final wages, made sure they had appropriate references, thanked them for their services and allowed them to leave a little early. The only servant left was Lakshmi.

Melanie grabbed her by the hand that morning and demanded to say goodbye to the elephants. Her mother agreed they could go, but that they must return within the hour because the taxi was coming to take them to the ship.

Giggling, the old Indian woman and the little English girl made their way to the Hanging Gardens for the last time. Melanie tugged at Lakshmi's hand, but soon realised that the ayah was struggling for breath. She slowed down and insisted that Lakshmi rest for a while. They had reached the rose garden, her favourite place in the park where a bench stood nearby. As Lakshmi sat to catch her breath, Melanie snuggled up to her, sucking her thumb as she did when she was in need of comfort. Reaching out, she took a lock of Lakshmi's hair and curled it round her finger.

"I love you, Lakshmi. I wish you could come with us to England."

"I love you too, Missybaba. But it is time for Lakshmi to retire."

"What's 'retire?'"

"To finish working. To rest."

"And where will you rest?"

"There is a most comfortable bed waiting for me in the hospital. Your father has made it available to me."

"Are you ill, Lakshmi?" The child's anxiety showed clearly. She stopped twisting Lakshmi's hair, took her hand and kissed her thumb.

"Only for a very little while," she said, knowing that her heart would not beat for much longer: already it was pumping too hard and she was feeling dizzy. But she had this last experience of love to take with her. "Only for a little while. And then I am being quite well again."

She was smiling down at Melanie when they heard a commotion. A high shrieking sound, and a thundering of feet. Instinctively, Lakshmi drew the child to her and pushed her up onto the bench beside her. Hardly had she heaved herself up, so that the two of them were standing side-by-side on the bench than the elephants burst through the gate into the rose garden.

Trumpeting loudly, their trunks thrown back and their short tusks much in evidence, the huge animals thundered past, the mahout swinging between them. He was shouting something but his words were impossible to catch. The elephants passed so close to the ayah and the child that Melanie thought she felt the rasp of elephant skin on hers. Next moment they were gone, leaving only the shock of their passing and a strong smell of elephant.

Melanie jumped down from the seat and turned to Lakshmi whose face had gone a strange pale colour, mostly grey. She helped her down and made her sit for a while, holding her hand and looking at her anxiously. Lakshmi's heart was thumping in her chest and for a while she sat with her head in her hands. Maybe it was a minute, maybe longer, but when she raised her head she realised that Melanie was rubbing her back and crooning — and what she was crooning was Ganesha's mantra. She felt better immediately: the Remover of Obstacles would help her to recover. She started chanting silently. When she raised her head, Melanie was looking into her eyes; and in those eyes she saw what she had craved all her life. She saw love: and in that moment knew that, at last, she was truly loved.

Now she must take the child home to her parents. After that, she might not need the hospital after all. She felt her death approaching: and she felt only relief and release. A time of rest. And then, perhaps, another life. But rest first. Rest — the bliss of it: a luxury she had not known in this life.

She raised herself to her feet, swayed for a moment, then: "Come," she said, "The elephants have gone. They have indeed given you a proper fanfare! Now we must go home."

A fanfare! The elephants knew she was going back to England. They had said farewell. And they had said it in a way that meant she could not be sad and cry. They had made a special event especially for her and she would remember it forever.

"Yes," she said, feeling oddly older than her years. "They have said goodbye. And now I must look after you, Lakshmi, and help you home."

So the old woman leaned on the little girl and they went slowly home.

Elizabeth was busy gathering all the last-minute oddments together.

"Daddy is in the taxi, waiting," she said. "Go and join him darling. I'll be there in a minute."

Lakshmi had gathered up her possessions and taken them out into the garden where she'd unrolled the bed roll on the grass by the rhododendrons and laid down on it.

Melanie saw her as she skipped towards the waiting taxi where her father was chatting with the driver. She looked at her father, a cigarette half-smoked in his hand, but he did not notice her.

She went to Lakshmi: the ayah's eyes were closed, but she was smiling. Melanie gently stroked the furrowed brow as Lakshmi had done for her. Then she leaned close and kissed her.

"Melanie! Where are you?" Her father's voice, impatient.

"Goodbye, Lakshmi. I love you." Melanie whispered in Lakshmi's ear so as not to disturb her.

Lakshmi's smile widened but she didn't open her eyes. Instead her mouth opened and she sighed.

Melanie adjusted Lakshmi's sari so she was comfortable.

"Melanie! Come on!"

A last glance. Lakshmi looked peaceful and her face had softened.

"Melanie!"

Lakshmi was sleeping: soon she would be well. Wasn't that what she had said when Melanie had the fever? 'You sleep now, Missy. In the morning, all will be well.'

The child ran to her parents. The taxi hooted as it moved away, and Melanie waved through the rear window, but Lakshmi did not stir. Melanie was sad and happy all in one. She was sad to be leaving Lakshmi behind, but she was glad that her ayah was sleeping. Soon she would be well again and would not have to go to hospital. Melanie knew Lakshmi would not like being in hospital because it was a disagreeable place that smelled horrible and didn't allow little girls to visit. Lakshmi had looked so very peaceful lying in the shade of the rhododendrons, but she would have liked her to have waved goodbye.

The taxi rounded the corner by the elephants' enclosure.

"Look Melanie! There are your elephant friends."

But Melanie was already looking — there they were, her great grey friends of the warm wrinkled skin and warm grey smell. How she loved them! And they were pressed up against the enclosure's fence, trunks delicately sniffing the air. They must know she was passing! She knelt up on the back seat and waved and waved until they were long out of sight. She sniffed her tears to the back of her nose.

"Let's sing the elephant song," Mummy suggested. "Nelly the elephant ..."

So they sang the elephant song over and over until Melanie was smiling again and then Mummy started telling her about all the exciting things they would do and see on the voyage back to England. Almost before she had finished speaking, they were boarding the ship that would carry them back to another continent and to another way of life.

Although she would never to return to the Indian sub-continent, it would always be remembered as a golden haze in Melanie's heart — the sunshine, The

Hanging Gardens, the elephants, the smells, the festival of Ganesha, the people — and above all, the warm loving heart of a giggly old Indian woman who wore a pink sari edged with gold.

Acknowledgements

Special thanks go to Dhivya Balaji and Shree Janani Sundararajan who reviewed a previous book of mine on their blog website: (readmuse.blogspot.co.uk) and, in doing so, earned not only my affection, but also my respect. In the course of subsequent conversations about books and reading, they each mentioned individually that they would like to read the story of my experience of elephants in India. I considered this for a while: then Shree Janini sent me a photograph of a temple elephant walking down a busy thoroughfare — and that was enough to set my memory whirring! The short story soon expanded to become a small book.

My husband, Richard Eaton has lived with the writer in me — not an easy task when my creative juices are in full flow — and helped me enormously in the editing and production of the final story. That does not mean that he is responsible for any of it: that responsibility rests on my shoulders alone! Thank you, Richard.

But most of all, thank you, my readers, for lending your eyes and ears to my story. I do hope you enjoyed reading it.

About the Author

As a small girl in the early nineteen fifties, Marion Eaton travelled to West Pakistan and India with her parents, her father being the appointed Resident Civil Engineer responsible for the construction of roads and tanks in those countries. To a child brought up in the green and leafy English countryside, the Indian Subcontinent and its people were as strange and exciting as they were fascinating. In Mumbai (then called Bombay) she found an affinity with the elephants of the Hanging Gardens on Malabar Hill and developed a great love for Lakshmi, the ayah she did her best to escape whenever she could.

She lives in the Sussex countryside with a very understanding husband, a very spoiled, lazy hound and a large rambling garden, all of which she attempts to keep in some semblance of order.

More information can be found at marioneaton.com.

A note from the Author

Thank you very much for reading my memoir. I do hope you enjoyed travelling to Karachi and Bombay with a six year old.

If you would like to receive the occasional newsletter, please sign up for one on marioneaton.com. You may also like to follow me on Twitter @marioneaton and/or like my Facebook page. I would love to hear from you. Please mention this book and I will be pleased to send you a free short story in appreciation.

You may not know that **honest reviews** are of **immense value** to an author so if you would give one on amazon.co.uk or amazon.com it would be of enormous help. And greatly appreciated. Thank you.

Other Books Published by Touchworks Ltd.

Print & e-books available from amazon.co.uk & amazon.com

Getting Ready to START A BUSINESS
by Richard Eaton

REVIEWS

"The most relevant business start-up book I have seen. In a few pages it reminds the reader of essential points and provides links to best practice. An excellent work. One to read before you start and to keep on the shelf for future reference."
CLIVE MARSH, Author
Financial Management for Non-Financial Managers
Business and Financial Models: Kogan Page

"A pocket-sized guide for aspiring entrepreneurs that links to valuable and reliable online information: a real help for those at the start of the business planning process."
IAN SMALLWOOD, Head of Business Services,
Let's Do Business Group

"Succinct points and clear advice in a neat package. If you are setting up your business this book tells you clearly the issues you face and how to start dealing with them. ... Great advice succinctly put, this guide sets out a clear framework, checklist and where to go next. It is useful for setting up any kind of business."
CATH TAJIMA-POWELL, Arts & Heritage Project Manager

"Essential reading for anyone who wants to start their own business."
CHARLOTTE ELFDAHL, Founder of Rockville Lampshades
Winner of 'Tomorrow's Business Builders Award 2013'

"A handy guide providing good background information to help you with taking the first steps in researching your business and writing your business plan"
KAYE CRITTELL of Let's Do Business Group

"A handy reference to guide you as you write your Business Plan and prepare to start up in business."
KEIR DELLAR, Head of Projects, Let's Do Business Group

When the Clocks Stopped
by **M.L. Eaton**

No 1 in the Mysterious Marsh Series

The long hot summer of 1976. The mysterious Romney Marsh in the South of England. Hazel Dawkins, a feisty young lawyer, takes maternity leave anticipating a period of tranquillity. Instead, the dreams begin. In them she encounters Annie, a passionate young woman whose romantic and tempestuous life was adventurously lived, more than two centuries previously, in the cottage that Hazel now occupies.

As their destinies entwine, Hazel not only confronts a terrifying challenge which parallels history, she finds herself desperately fighting for survival in a cruel and unforgiving age. Even more disturbing is the realisation that her battle will affect the future for those in the past whose fate is, as yet, unwritten.

Her only ally is Annie. Together they face events that echo through the centuries, events that are as violent and compelling as they are unexpected.

And, as the past collides with the present, the time for the birth of Hazel's child draws ever nearer.

When the Tide Turned
by **M.L. Eaton**

No 2 in the Mysterious Marsh Series

It is August 1976 and an oppressive heat hangs over Romney Marsh in the South East corner of England.

Soon after the birth of her daughter, Hazel Dawkins, a young lawyer, is unexpectedly asked to return to work. No sooner has she agreed than she discovers that a dark force threatens both her family and her country; and before long, the past and present intertwine in a rising tide of horrifying events.

Haunted by terrifying images, she knows that she must uncover secrets from the past if she is to avert a catastrophe that will destroy all that she holds dear.

What draws her to the painting depicting a sudden storm at sea on a night in 1803 as Napoleon prepares to invade England?

What is the secret of the man pegged down to die on the incoming tide?

As Hazel seeks the answers to these questions, she faces evil and intrigue, her life and that of her baby daughter, threatened at every turn.

A Taste of

When the Clocks Stopped

Prologue

The silver light of a gibbous moon shimmers on the new green leaves of the ash tree. The horse stamps and jerks his head, jangling the bridle. I sway with the movement, soothing him instinctively. The sweetish smell of horse is thick about me as I wait at the crossroads. Stiff as I am in every joint and sinew, my body screams for me to dismount and stretch my legs, but I cannot. Some intuition, some sense of impending destiny, holds me motionless. I am aware it will not be long.

I flinch as the expectant hush is broken by the screech of an owl, eerie in the stillness that binds me to the saddle. She circles silently above me, seeking her prey. I watch until she glides away into the blackest shadows, where the sacred ash grove huddles beneath the escarpment.

My eyes seek the hallowed place where the Earth Mother is still honoured by man and maid on the sacred feast of Beltane; the ash grove to which they come at dawn, clad in white, and garlanded in green. May blossoms wreathe their brows as they stand side by side under a living canopy for their hand-clasping, their ceremony of rejoicing in union, the celebration of life itself in dance and song. This is the seven-treed sacred grove to which my beloved and I came not long ago; there we swore an oath to honour our love and there later, alone beneath the moon-silvered leaves we became one in the flesh.

It grows cold now, and I shiver. The horse pricks up his ears, listening intently. A small sound trembles towards me; perhaps no more than a fluctuation in the air current. Then the nightingale's exquisite song fills the air with beauty. It is the signal:Jack's signal.

I fire my weapon into the sky and wheel about, pulling sharply on the reins. We race off into the night. Lying close to the horse's back, my head beside his ear, I ride hard. For a moment or two, as we gather speed, I choose those places where the low light gleams through the covering of cloud. I catch the sound of hooves in swift pursuit and know I have been seen. Now I guide my good companion into the gloom of the darkest shadows, allowing him to choose his own footing on the causeway. He gallops on.

I risk a backward glimpse. Shapes pursue us; legless in the mist rising from the Marsh, centaurs ride hard in a bow-shaped line. The triumph and excitement of the men who chase me is almost palpable. How long were they lingering near the crossroads where I myself had waited?

I let the gelding have his head because he knows these levels well. His hooves drum into the earth and I crouch low in the saddle, horse sweat hot-smelling in my nostrils. As I cling to his mane, I chance another glance but see nothing. I am sure we are gaining on our pursuers, but have they ridden yet into the trap where the Marsh is quicksand and will swallow horse and rider whole?

The moon is hidden now and I have no bearings. All I hear is a thrumming, thrumming, thrumming — and I know not whether it is my heart beating in my ears or the sound of pursuit. All I can do is ride.

Made in the USA
Charleston, SC
04 June 2016